Mary Elizabeth Fraser-Tytler

Grisel Romney

A Novel: Vol. II

Mary Elizabeth Fraser-Tytler

Grisel Romney
A Novel: Vol. II

ISBN/EAN: 9783337045180

Printed in Europe, USA, Canada, Australia, Japan

Cover: Foto ©Andreas Hilbeck / pixelio.de

More available books at **www.hansebooks.com**

GRISEL ROMNEY

A Novel

BY

M. E. FRASER-TYTLER

IN TWO VOLUMES
VOL. II.

"So young and so untender?"
"So young, my lord, and true."
KING LEAR, *Act I.*

London:
MARCUS WARD & CO., 67, 68, CHANDOS STREET
AND ROYAL ULSTER WORKS, BELFAST
1880

CONTENTS.

GRISEL ROMNEY.

CHAPTER I.

PICKING UP THE THREADS.

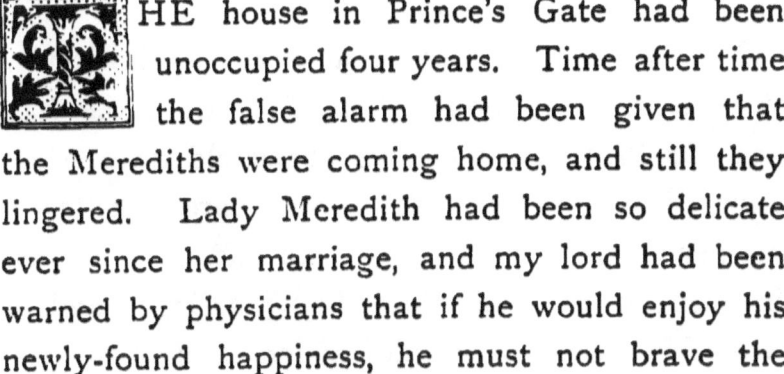 HE house in Prince's Gate had been unoccupied four years. Time after time the false alarm had been given that the Merediths were coming home, and still they lingered. Lady Meredith had been so delicate ever since her marriage, and my lord had been warned by physicians that if he would enjoy his newly-found happiness, he must not brave the inclemencies of British climate.

A son had been born to them some two years after their marriage, so Lord Meredith wandered from place to place with his wife and child, seeking for health for the former. As years went by, she was growing more precious to him; his heart stopped with a sudden spasm when, at times, the idea presented itself to him that he might be left alone before long. How could he ever live without her? How could he bring up the child as she would wish? He so ignorant and useless in all such things.

But Lenore did not die; gradually she rallied from the shock occasioned by her father's death; such was the physicians' report, and she did not contradict them. Mercifully for her, the reason seemed a likely one, and she was allowed to go on her way unquestioned.

Now, at last, they were at home again. How strange it all seemed! The first time she had been in Prince's Gate since those old days when another was there also! She dare not for a moment look into the past; she had never visited it even in thought since her marriage, and it was this ceaseless strain which had done the mischief—the constant watchfulness lest she should prove untrue to the man whom she had promised to love, honour, and obey above all others.

It was the day after their arrival in London. Lenore was sitting alone. She had not been out; she was recovering from the effects of her journey.

Lord Meredith had gone to his club. It was about five o'clock in the afternoon, the time of year February. London was empty, Easter was early, and everyone was still out of town. Lent was going on. What need to be there when there were no amusements to tempt the public. So hunting boxes were crowded all over England, and in the metropolis the unworldly kept their fast.

Lenore's busy fingers were embroidering some article of clothing for her boy. She used to hate work, but she had grown to love it—it stopped thought. Overhead, in the nursery, she heard his merry feet pattering, a smile came into her face, she rose from her chair, and was about to send a message that he should be brought to her.

She hesitated a moment; a ring at the doorbell, then the servant entered with a card, asking if she were too tired to see the gentleman.

"Not at all; show Mr. Jerningham upstairs."

Philip must have already been there, for he entered immediately.

"I could not resist coming," he said. "I chanced upon Lord Meredith on the way to his club, and he gave me leave to visit you. You must send me away if I am too much for you."

B

"Indeed it was kind of you to come to see us so soon. No, you will not tire me in the least. Sit down and tell me all about yourself since I last saw you, and your sister also ; it is such a time since I have heard anything of her. Is she still Miss Jerningham, or has she changed her name for another?"

"Oh, Augusta is still Augusta Jerningham. That's the harm in being an heiress, Lady Meredith. When Augusta's aunt left her all her money, and passed your humble servant over, she did her incalculable mischief. She might have been married, with all the joys of a large family and poverty, had it not been for her money, which makes her look on the most innocent as fortune-hunting."

"And where is she at present—in town?"

"Well, she was never famous at letter-writing ; but, as far as I know, she is with our old friend Mrs. Wyld just now ; after that she is going to the Romneys, and I join her there."

"Romney! Surely that was the name of two elderly ladies I knew at Brighton. Are they new acquaintances, Mr. Jerningham? We have lived so utterly out of the way, that I feel an absolute ignoramus on all questions relating to my friends."

"Not exactly new friends, Lady Meredith. There are three daughters, and you see—I suppose I may as well tell you—I am going to be married to one of them."

"Are you? I am very glad; but tell me more. The name seems familiar to me; where can I have heard it?"

"Perhaps in connection with the youngest, Grisel. She is engaged to a mutual old friend of ours, Jack Hunt."

Philip looked past Lenore; he wished to give the information; he almost felt the start she gave, though he did not see it.

She did not answer at first, but leant forward and poked the fire. The tremble of her voice was imperceptible as she asked—

"How long has Mr. Hunt been engaged? You must wish him happiness from me when you see him."

"Will you not wish it him yourself, Lady Meredith? He is in town, and will doubtless come and see you whenever he hears of your arrival, but congratulations are no new thing to him. They have been engaged four years."

"And why have they never married?"

"First one thing and then another. Miss Grisel

Romney was too young, and would not give her
consent; she put it off from month to month, and
latterly Jack has not pressed it. He is frightfully
busy; within the last two years he seems only
to live for work. He has much changed since
the old days, Lady Meredith; does not go into
society at all, and never takes a holiday, save
for a hurried run down to the Manor to see his
fiancée."

"What is Miss Romney like?" Lenore asked.
Could it have been she whom she met with
him the last time she ever saw Jack?

"Small, and neither fair nor dark, with eyes
and mouth usually smiling. I do not wonder
at his falling into her toils."

The description answered perfectly; of course
it was easily explained—she must have been
staying with her aunts at Brighton.

"And your Miss Romney, what of her? Tell
me of your lady-love."

"She's one in a thousand in every way; but
I will not describe her to you. She and Grisel
are in town just now, staying in Cavendish
Square. I may bring them to see you?"

"I should like to make their acquaintance,"
Lenore answered very quietly, "if they will not

think it too formidable, coming without further introduction ; but I fear I am not strong enough to pay ceremonious visits."

"What a duffer I am, to be sure. Here have I been sitting all this time, and not asked after your health. I was awfully sorry to hear you had been so far from strong. Are you really better now ?"

"Yes, much better, thank you. But my health is an uninteresting topic ; I would much rather hear all about your future."

"Oh, our future is all cut and dry. Mr. Wyld's land-stewardship has fallen vacant, and he has offered it to me. Just suits me to a nicety, and Bryde is quite satisfied."

"Bryde ! Is that your *fiancée?* What a quaint name. How do she and her sister come to have such nice old names ?"

"Some legend in the annals of the Romneys ; but I cannot tell you just now. I hear Lord Meredith's voice, and I fear he will give me notice to quit."

"No, no ; our chat has done me good. Here you are ?" she said, looking round as Lord Meredith entered the room.

"Well, are you pleased with the visitor I

found for you? I thought you would like to talk over old days when I was out of the way. Now, don't move, Jerningham; we have not been at home long enough yet for me to have made a particular chair my own. You are not over-tired, Lenore, are you?"

"No; on the contrary, I am wonderfully fresh to-night. Mr. Jerningham has been telling me a piece of news, Fred. He is going to be married!"

"Following our good example—eh, Lenore? My best wishes for your happiness. And who may the happy lady be?"

"Rather, I am the happy man! Is not that a good amendment, Lady Meredith? Bryde Romney is her name; I hope you will soon make her acquaintance."

Philip sat for some little while longer. Lenore enjoyed talking with him, he was so exactly the Philip of old days, with the same fresh vehemence in all he did and said. He would not rest satisfied till Lenore appointed an hour for him the following day to bring Bryde and her sister to make her acquaintance.

At last the clock striking warned him of the flight of time, and he rose to take his departure.

"I shall meet Jack Hunt this evening. May I

tell him you would like to see him—that you are once more settled in town?"

"If Mr. Hunt cares to renew an old friendship, I shall be very glad to see him. Tell him I shall be at home any afternoon after four o'clock; but do not make him feel obliged to come; if he is so occupied, he may not care to give any of his valuable spare time away."

"Perhaps you are right," Philip answered, wondering if he had been wrong in making the suggestion. That Jack and Lenore had made a mistake in their lives he was sure; the subject had often puzzled him; it occupied his mind now as he hurried to his rooms to dress for the early dinner in Cavendish Square.

Lord Meredith having dismissed Philip returned to the drawing-room. He sank into his chair with a sigh of satisfaction. Lenore looked up and smiled.

"There's no place like home," he said; "not but that I have enjoyed my years of Continental wandering," he added, dreading to leave an impression that he had wearied of his forced life abroad.

Lenore read the motive which prompted his remark, she had learnt to know him so thoroughly; and he, reserved to others, delighted all the more in the fact that she read him through and through.

"If you are glad to have a settled home," she answered, "what must I be? Remember, this is my first home since I was twelve years old; half my life wandering about—such a time ago it seems."

"You are getting such an old woman, Lenore." He was smiling at her earnestness. "To think of having lived twenty-four years. It *is* a lifetime. Add twenty-four to that, and we have forty-eight. Still two years too few. Your boy's age must be added also, child; and then do you see what an old man you have for——"

"Hush!" she said, rising from her chair and laying her delicately-veined hand upon his mouth. He drew her gently down to him and kissed her.

"So you do not like arithmetic, child," he said.

"I am not going to be teased; you are driving me away," she said.

"To your boy, I suppose. I shall grow jealous."

"I am not the least afraid," she answered, laughing, as she left the room.

Lord Meredith raised a book from the table. He did not read much. Gradually the shadows deepened in the room. It was intensely comfortable after the damp, cold fog of the February afternoon. There certainly was no place like home. In about five minutes he was sound asleep.

Lenore, returning shortly afterwards, opened the door softly and stole away again to her room. Philip Jerningham's information was constantly before her. She longed and yet dreaded to see Jack. Why should I care so much? she wondered. I, an old married woman, and he engaged to a girl for four years. Surely by this time we can meet without being haunted by the past.

Philip had told Lenore that he would meet Jack that evening.

On arriving at Cavendish Square he found he was the only addition to the three ladies. Miss Romney's health was failing; she went early to her room. Miss Griselda and her two nieces made up the quartette.

No one was in the room when Philip arrived, but Bryde made her appearance before long.

"Grisel has had a disappointment to-night," she

said. "Jack is too busy to dine with us. I cannot understand what occupies him so constantly."

"His writing, I believe. He is doing too much. I must look in and give him a word on the subject on my way home to-night."

"It is of no use; we have all done our best. Fortunately, Grisette does not mind as some people would. She is of such a sunny nature, that it takes a great deal to damp her spirits."

"When are they going to be married, Bryde? Lady Meredith asked me the question this afternoon."

"Some time in autumn, Grisel says. But tell me about the Merediths. I did not know you were going to see them."

"Neither did I. I accidentally met Lord Meredith, and thought I could not do better than use up my unemployed afternoon in paying my respects to his wife. If you will go and make engagements in which I have no part, so must I."

"It was not my fault, Philip. I was the victim of circumstances, for which read dressmaker. However, I have something to ask you about. Did you ever hear before that Grisel's Jack was an old admirer of Lady Meredith?"

" What put that into your head, Bryde ?"

" Something Augusta said to me one day."

" Augusta should learn to be silent."

" But why ? Lady Meredith was engaged to be married long before Grisel knew Jack, only I wondered that he never spoke of the Fentons. Was there anything really in it ?"

" Look here, Bryde, I may as well tell you, but I wish Augusta would learn to hold her tongue. Jack Hunt and Lenore Fenton were great allies in the old days. At one time I never doubted that it would all come right. Then something came between them, I have never found out what ; but Miss Fenton's marriage was announced imme- diately after, and Jack came to you, and in ten days was engaged to Grisel."

" And didn't care a bit about her. How could he do such a thing, Phil ? Poor Grisette !"

" I am sure he liked Grisette also ; but I cannot make it out. There was a mystery somewhere. Sir James Fenton could have solved it, I think, or Lady Meredith ; and she never will."

" And Grisette is to be the victim of their mysteries !" exclaimed Bryde, indignantly.

" What a fiery creature you are, Miss Bridget. Remember, you and I would never have had the extreme felicity of seeing so much of each other had it not been for Jack's little mistake. But hush! here's Grisette. Keep all the surmises I have told you under lock and key."

Grisel's voice was heard singing as she descended the staircase; a rich, soft contralto, everyone must be struck with its freshness and beauty. A moment afterwards she entered the room dressed in something white; she could hardly ever be induced to wear anything else. She looked very little older than she did four years ago, and had the same unconventional way in all she did and said.

"Well, Grisette, I hear you are in low spirits to-night at Jack playing truant."

"Isn't it stupid of him? I see so little of him now!"

"You will have to consent to his wishes, Miss Griselda, and then you will see more of him."

"But I do so hate housekeeping, Phil. Sybil says I must learn, and I have never even begun yet. It seems so ridiculous to think of me being a married woman. I am not nearly tired of fun yet!"

"And what does Jack say to all these excuses? Do you know, Grisette, I am sorry for him?"

"Sorry for Jack! Surely not. It must be much better for him that I should gain some experience, and not try experiments upon him. Do you really mean, Philip, that you are sorry for him?"

"Yes, I am sorry for him, for I think he is working too hard, and if he had you to look after him it would be different. Do you not notice that he is growing quite grey? It is simply from so much thought, and no one to cheer him between times."

"And bald, also," said Grisel, meditatively. "I never thought of it in that light before. I will speak seriously to him about it to-morrow, and then, if I can do any good, I will make up my mind to the housekeeping."

CHAPTER II.

SIMPLY A MATTER OF BUSINESS.

IT was the same evening as Philip dined in Cavendish Square; Jack Hunt had just finished dinner, and was sitting ruminating in a comfortable chair before the fire. Not a very inviting room, somehow; the walls covered with a dun-coloured flock paper, and the carpet brilliant in scarlets and green in gigantic designs. The mantelpiece had the usual gilt clock, which pointed to the hour of nine, flanked by match-boxes and vases, splendid specimens of provincial potteries. A side-table and several chairs groaned under the weight of books and periodicals. The maid was clearing away the dinner things, and Jack fidgeted impatiently — the clatter of dishes was overpowering.

Certainly the years past had left their stamp pretty plainly on him. His face had grown sterner, harder; he was also, as Grisel remarked, growing bald, and streaks of grey were visible.

To say that his unfortunate love of four years ago had occasioned this change would not be true; it certainly, however, originated it; but "man's love is of man's life a thing apart," and it had taken hours of work and study before such outward traces were visible.

He had made some money by his work; he was no longer straitened in his means; he had made a name for himself in the literary world; he had succeeded in everything he undertook but one— he had never made Grisel love him. At first he thought it would be easy, she was such a child; but he had grown almost hopeless now, and as the months ran on, her love was becoming more and more necessary to him—he had grown to long for it. His business life was eating the freshness out of his existence; he craved for some strong counteracting influence.

At first he had taken to work to drown thought; he continued it now from habit, and from a certain satisfaction in gratifying his ambition.

This evening his mind was occupied; he had written a much-talked-of article in a leading journal. The name of the author had leaked out, and he had been congratulated on all hands that day.

Grisel knew nothing of it ; at first, she read his articles from a sense of duty, but he rarely told her of them now. Why should she read that which was so irksome to her? She had never said such was the case; on the contrary, she read everything she knew he had written with patient care, till one day Tom exclaimed, in Jack's presence, "Is your task finished yet, La Grise?" "Very nearly now," she answered, and shortly after flung down the magazine with a sigh of relief. After she left the room, Jack found it was his last article she had been reading.

He had kept his writings since then more to himself, but this particular evening he was overpowered with a longing for sympathy in his work. The praise of the world was nothing to the praise of one. His thoughts were leading him into the "what-might-have-beens"—always a most dangerous and unprofitable region—when a knock came at the door. Could Mr. Hunt see a gentleman who had called on business? Of course he could ; it would be about some of his editorial work.

He was right, for the next hour he was fully

occupied ; at last the work was done, and Mr.
Strange and he dropped into ordinary conversation—of the events of the day, of the money
market, &c. A good deal of uneasiness had been
experienced by the collapse of two large firms ;
there was grave subject for conjecture.

Jack had been making some fresh investments.
He took the opportunity to riddle Mr. Strange's
brains, as he was more up in such things than
Hunt himself.

"Did you ever meet a man I saw in the street
to-day—Lord Meredith ?" asked Mr. Strange.

"Some years ago I was in the same room with
him once or twice. I understood he was abroad."

" So did I, till to-day. What makes me ask is
his connection with this panic. He suffered pretty
severely some four years ago at the time railways
were in such a bad way."

" That was—— ?"

" Just before his marriage. I happen to know
all about it ; rather a strange story ; but it oozed
out to me through my father-in-law, who was
Meredith's man of business."

" And so the story has become public property,"
Jack answered sharply.

" No harm in repetition now ; the principal
c

actor is dead. From all one hears of Sir James
Fenton, he cannot have had much of a character."

"You had better tell me the whole thing, now
you have begun." Jack spoke impatiently; a
conviction was rising in his mind that he was
going to hear something of personal interest.

"Are you interested in the actors?" he asked.

Mr. Strange looked questioningly at his listener.

"I knew Sir James Fenton some years ago, and
his daughter."

"Then you knew some one worth knowing.
Lady Meredith must be, from all one hears, no
ordinary woman."

"But this has nothing to do with Lord Meredith's loss. Lady Meredith was only a girl when
I knew her."

"It has to do with it in a way. My father-in-
law saw a good deal of her at the time of her
father's death, and it is his conviction that she
married the wrong man."

"Idle conjecture! People are so ready to
attribute motives where none existed. A coronet
and wealth, added to unexceptional personal
worth, is rarely the wrong man."

"Well, judge for yourself. In the spring of
four years ago, my father-in-law, Mr. Harvey, was

sent for one day to see Sir James, at the time
staying under Lord Meredith's roof.   Sir James
had got into difficulties.   He had contracted large
debts as a young man, and they had fallen due.
There was no money to meet them.   I don't
know all the ins and outs, but it resulted in Lord
Meredith advancing the money—in fact, he set
Sir James straight, and then married his daughter."

"And did Miss Fenton know anything of this?"

"At the time Mr. Harvey understood she did
not.   From an allusion she made after her father's
death, asking about the possibility of the liquida-
tion of debt to Lord Meredith, she must have been
in the secret."

"You believe, then, she married Lord Meredith,
being under such obligation to him.   Pleasant for
her husband!   The world was kind enough to
impute other motives to her."

"The world has usually got some theory.   After
all, it is simply conjecture what I have now told
you.   Sir James died at Brighton.   His daughter
at once sent for Mr. Harvey.   It was not till after
the funeral she even saw Lord Meredith, though
he also was in Brighton.   When my father-in-law
saw her first, she was full of some project of living
on a hundred pounds a-year, allowed to her from

her uncle's estates, and indefinitely postponing her
marriage.   However, she soon changed her mind.
I suppose it did not sound so tempting on con-
sideration ; so she did wisely, and made up her
mind to the marriage."

Jack remained absolutely silent.   Mr. Strange
rose to go.

" I have given you a long, gossiping history,
Hunt, all brought on by this crisis in connection
with Lord Meredith.   It was depression in
American stocks which brought Sir James Fenton
to grief."

" And you say the Merediths are back in
town ?"

" Yes ; I saw him to-day.   You had better renew
your acquaintance with them ; only, remember
that you are no wiser than the rest of the world."
Such were Mr. Strange's parting words, and Jack
was alone.

He had suffered keenly during the last half-
hour.   He had certainly never counted on gaining
the explanation of Lenore's marriage in the way
he had done.   And instead of satisfaction and
justification of his own line of conduct, he saw
how madly he had acted.   The last time he had
spoken with her came back to his mind ; and

even in the water-colour gallery some foreshadow-
ing of what was coming wrung from her the words,
"Duty might demand the sacrifice of self."
Words and actions passed over at the time were
now pregnant with meaning. How had he been
so blinded by his wounded self-love? Then his
subsequent conduct—the unseemly haste with
which he had· wooed and won Grisel, when at
the time he had absolutely no heart to bestow.
Fate had used him a thousand times better than
he deserved. The thought of Grisel always
brought sunshine with it; he certainly, for the
second time, had drawn a prize in life's lottery.

He was not destined to be long alone that
evening, his meditations were again interrupted.
Philip, without warning, invaded his room. He
was on his way home from Cavendish Square, and
was the bearer of a message from Grisel.

"Really this is too bad!" he exclaimed. "I
thought you could not dine with us to-night
because of work, and I find you absolutely
idle, without a trace of occupation of any kind
about."

"The excuse was a valid one, all the same.
My evening has been interrupted once already;
·I had not been alone five minutes when you came

in. The work must be done some time to-night, however."

"Which means that my absence would be better than my presence."

"No; not at all. Sit down, and give me news of Grisel, as I fear I shall not see her till late to-morrow."

"That will suit admirably. She was afraid you might want her in the afternoon, and I have promised she should go with me to see Lady Meredith."

"I heard they had come to town. Does Lady Meredith know in what relation I stand to Grisel?"

Jack spoke gravely.

Philip answered, "Yes, I told her everything. She sent you her kindest congratulations, and hopes you will go and see her."

"I do not see the use of it. We have not met for so long, it is better to let our acquaintance be a thing of the past."

"But such cannot be. She wishes to know Bryde and Grisel. She was most minute in her inquiries about the latter. I have promised to take them both to Prince's Gate to-morrow."

"Is Lady Meredith much changed?"

"Changed! Not the least in the world. In one

way she's changed—looks delicate and moves languidly ; and you remember in the old days what an elastic spring she had when she walked. Otherwise, just like Lenore Fenton. You must go and see her, Jack ; she would be hurt if you didn't."

" I am not sure. I hate making new acquaintances."

" Look here, Hunt," said Philip. " Once on a time I thought things would have been very different. You made a mess of it somehow. But whether I am right or wrong in my conjectures, it can never do a man anything but good to know Lenore Meredith."

Philip spoke very earnestly. He did not expect an answer. There was silence for some minutes. Jack sat gazing moodily into the fire ; Philip was watching the smoke curl lazily from their cigars. At last he broke the silence.

" There was a letter from Sybil to-night. Old Sir Roger Mainwaring is far from well."

" Seriously ill, or only one of his usual fits of gout ?"

" It must be something serious, I imagine, for their son is coming home from India for a year."

" Le Gris coming home ! What does Grisel say ?"

The words broke from Jack's lips before he
was aware. "They were old playfellows, you
know, as children," he added, by way of explanation.

"Yes, I know. But Grisette's feelings seemed
to be of a mixed character—her sympathies were
divided between sorrow for Lady Mainwaring and
the pleasure of seeing Reggie again. He was, at
any rate, to have come next year. It is only that
he has hurried his movements."

"Then do you suppose that there is cause for
uneasiness more than usual—that Sir Roger is in
immediate danger? One result of his death would
be Reggie's succession to the baronetage and
estates. There is no other son, is there?"

"No; he is an only child. I suppose he would
leave the army and settle at the Hall. Probably
marry in time. It would be a great thing for
the Romneys if the future Lady Mainwaring were
the right sort. With such near neighbours it is
of consequence."

Conversation flagged again. Philip would not
have prolonged his stay, had it not been for a hope
that he might rouse Jack from his evident fit of
depression. The clock, with various previous
warnings, slowly struck twelve. Jack glanced at

it somewhat vacantly, and compared it with his own watch.

"It is right for once," he said. "You must go, I fear, Phil. I must settle to work."

"You are working too hard, Jack. When are you and Grisel going to be married? You require a wife to keep you from overtaxing your brains."

"Nonsense!" laughed Jack. "I am all right. It would be dull work for poor Grisette looking after the health of my brains."

"In my opinion, you are quite wrong. Grisette is not liable to low spirits ; and besides, certainly I think you ought to be married soon—at any rate, before autumn."

Jack looked questioningly at Philip. Did he mean anything by what he said ?

"You are of opinion that our marriage should take place before autumn—before young Mainwaring comes home ?"

"This is really too much of a joke! I meant nothing of the kind. Fortunately, Grisel is not here, or she might have some ground for supposing that you were tired of the whole business. However, I am not going to quarrel with you, and as there seems no chance of making you hear reason to-night, I am going. Remember, Grisel expects you between five and six to-morrow, and if you take my advice, you will settle something definitely."

So Philip left, and Jack wrote on into the early hours of the morning.

CHAPTER III.

GRISETTE.

Ɏ ENORE was at home. It was the hour Philip Jerningham had promised to bring the Romneys to make her acquaintance; she was almost repenting of her resolution now, but it was too late to draw back.

Presently the door opened, and she was face to face with Grisel Romney. She knew at once which was which of the sisters, though Philip's introduction would not have left her long in doubt.

"I think this is not the first time I have seen you," she said, as, having shaken hands with Bryde, she turned to meet Grisel. "You and your sister were at the opera one night some four years ago, and Mr. Jerningham then pointed you out to me."

"And also once at Brighton," exclaimed Grisel, "we met you." Suddenly she came to a pause;

a recollection of Lenore's deep mourning, and the apparent marks of agitation at the time of meeting, reminded her she was treading on dangerous ground, but Lenore finished the sentence for her.

"Yes; I met you in the lanes at Brighton, when I was taking a solitary walk soon after my father's death; but you were not solitary," she added, smiling. "You must let me congratulate you, Miss Romney. Mr. Hunt is a very old friend of mine."

"Jack told me so at the time. He had so many friends before I knew him; but he is so busy, he has rarely time to tell me any of his past life."

Lenore turned away suddenly; she had the excuse of saying something to Bryde about her marriage, so they relapsed into general talk.

Lenore made herself very charming. Both girls fell in love with her at once. They thought the visit had been far too short when Philip, glancing at the clock, reminded Grisel she had promised to be at home at five. The girls rose to their feet. Bryde held out her hand with her usual frankness. "Grisel and I may come and see you again some day, may not we?"

"You must come often. Considering how long

I have known Mr. Jerningham, there is nothing
I should like better than also to be friends with his
future wife."

Then Lenore turned to Grisel and took both her
hands a moment in hers.

"Will you tell Mr. Hunt he must come and see
me?" she said, "or I will think that he has forgotten me."

Grisel's eyes looked frankly into Lenore's,
betraying such undisguised admiration of the
beautiful Lady Meredith. Her golden hair strayed
over her forehead from underneath her fur-trimmed
hat, and the excitement of the moment had
brought the colour into her face. A very charming face, Lenore thought, and she involuntarily
stooped and kissed her.

A moment after, she held out her hand to
Philip. "Good-bye," she said. Another minute,
and she was alone.

When Lord Meredith shortly after entered the
room, he was struck by Lenore's looking more
than ordinarily weary. She complained of head-
ache, but said nothing more was amiss. He would
not let her go down to the dining-room, and
several times during the evening she caught him
glancing furtively at her over his book. He told

her she had been doing too much, and that he would have to limit the number of people she saw.

Lenore laughed, and then she repeated to him most of what had passed that afternoon while the Romneys were with her.

"Do you remember meeting Mr. Hunt once here, long ago, at tea?" she at last asked her husband.

"Yes; very well. I took a great fancy to him at the time. Has he also been with you to-day?"

"Oh no; only he is engaged to be married to the youngest of the Miss Romneys—Grisel. I sent him a message by her to come and renew his acquaintance."

"Will be very glad to see him, Lenore. Make him more welcome perhaps even than in the old days," he added, with a light-hearted laugh. "It shows how much one is mistaken at times, but I then had a fancy that you and he cared for each other, but your father undeceived me on that score, and his assurance to the contrary made me the happy man I now am."

"Tied to a sick wife," said Lenore, summoning a smile to her quivering lips. It was hard to lie still on the sofa with her husband's eyes watching her with so much concern and anxiety in them, and to smile over the story of the part her dead father played in her life's history.

"My conviction that I was right had at one time almost reached certainty," Lord Meredith continued, happy in the thought that he had been mistaken. "When I tried to buy that picture, do you remember, in the water-colour exhibition, which had such a strong resemblance to you, and I found that a Mr. Hunt had been before me, immediately I put two and two together, and, man-like, came to a wrong conclusion. But you should go to your room, Lenore; I am over-tiring you," he said, as he saw a slight contraction in his wife's forehead.

"Perhaps I had better do so, Fred; my head is very bad to-night. I am but a sorry companion for you."

She rose languidly from the sofa, and he followed her to her room, carrying her shawl and pillows.

"Give me a kiss," she said, as he prepared to leave her. "Don't fret about me, Fred; I shall be all right again to-morrow."

So he left her to fight a battle alone that he, unsuspectingly, had made so much harder. It is difficult at times to annihilate the past.

Meanwhile, Grisel had gone home with her head full of Lady Meredith.

Jack found her in the firelight some half-hour afterwards. She was sitting on the rug, but sprang to her feet as he entered.

"Here you are at last," she exclaimed.

"Did you think I was late?" he asked, with a hope rising within him that at last she was going to care for him—that he was becoming necessary to her.

"I have been longing for you to come," she answered, "I have so much to tell you about. Where do you think we have been? You need not try to guess, but it was to see some one who sent a message to you."

"Tell me, Grisette, and put me out of pain."

"Have you no idea? Did not Philip tell you where he was going to take us to-day? We made acquaintance with 'a very old friend of yours,' that was what Lady Meredith called you. How beautiful she is, Jack! I wonder so much that you, who once knew her well, do not often speak of her. I do not think if I had ever known her I could have forgotten her."

"I have not forgotten her, Grisette; it would be impossible to do that; but when Lenore Fenton

became Lady Meredith her life turned into a
different channel, and so we have not met for
years."

"Perhaps it is as well for me," said Grisel,
meditatively; "I might have grown jealous. Do
you know, Jack, I believe if I had been a man I
should have fallen·in love with her. I wonder
you didn't."

Jack made no answer; Grisel thought he did
not hear what she said. He was sitting on a low
chair before the fire, and she knelt beside him, her
elbows resting on his knee. She put up one of
her hands and stroked his forehead.

"You are looking tired to-night, Jack. What
have you been doing to-day?"

"Nothing more than usual; but the firelight
and this comfortable chair make one lazy."

"You are working too hard just now; you will
be ill if you do not take care. I know I am
right."

Grisel spoke with an air of grave authority; she
felt she had Philip's opinion to fall back upon if
her own arguments failed.

"What has made you such an anxious little
woman all of a sudden? Who put such ideas
into your head?"

D

"Suppose they came of themselves, Jack. Do you think I am so very childish and foolish that I can think no careful thoughts about your health without some one having put them there?"

"I think you are a prodigy of wisdom," he answered, trying to treat her earnestness lightly. "What does your ladyship recommend that I should do to regain my shattered energies?"

"Don't laugh at me," she said, shyly holding down her head and playing with one of the buttons on his coat. "I really am trying to grow wise."

"You are wise enough for me, Grisette; and if I am content, what does it signify about the rest of the world?"

"But are you really content?" she asked, raising her eyes joyfully to his; "for if you think I would do just as I am, wouldn't it be better that we should be married soon, and then you would have me to take care of you?"

"Are you in earnest, child?" Jack exclaimed. "Would you not mind it very much? Do you really mean what you say?"

Grisel's eyes were very pleading as she answered, "I am in sober earnest. I do not look as if I were joking, do I? I was thinking of it seriously last night when you didn't come to dinner and spent a long evening alone at work, so I determined to tell you to-day that I think it ought to be soon."

"What do you call soon — some time in autumn?"

"Oh, before autumn. In summer, don't you think—perhaps about the end of June? I am going home, you know, in a few days, and I shall begin to learn housekeeping at once. I think I ought to know enough by summer."

"Your establishment will not be a very large one," he said, laughing, and stroking her hair, "and I will not be a very exacting critic if you do make mistakes at first."

"I promise to do my very best, and you will be there to tell me when I do wrong. It will not be as if I had to do it all alone. How very odd it will feel having you always there. Will you not be inclined to laugh at the idea of me being a married woman?"

Grisel pronounced the last words with a solemnity which was irresistible.

Jack put his arms round her and drew her closer to him. She nestled her head on his shoulder, she felt so pleased she had found courage to suggest their speedy marriage to him.

"Are you glad, Jack?" she asked, glancing up at him from under her long dark eyelashes.

"Very glad, Grisette," and then there was silence for some time.

But it was not in Grisel's nature to remain very long without talking. She raised her head from its resting-place, and sat down on the stool at Jack's feet.

"Have you heard that Le Gris is coming home?" she asked.

"Yes; Philip told me so. Are you very glad, La Grise?"

"Happier than I can tell you. It has seemed such a long time since he went away. We were always together; it was natural I should miss him!"

"And natural also that you should be glad to see him again. Have you heard how Sir Roger is?"

"Not to-day. Poor old Sir Roger! I hope there is no immediate danger. I do not know what Lady Mainwaring would do if Sir Roger died before Reggie came home. It would be different if she had a daughter, but even I am

away, and I used to be a kind of daughter to her.
She and Sir Roger always called me their adopted
daughter. I was more at the Hall than at home
when we were children."

"Lady Mainwaring must make the most of
you, Grisette, for the next few months. I fear
she will not approve of your new arrangements;
she will miss your constant visits."

"She will get accustomed to it soon; and,
besides, by that time she will have Reggie, and
you need me a great deal more than she does.
There is no chance of Lady Mainwaring over-
working her brains."

"You have quite made up your mind, I see,
to be head keeper of my brains. Remember,
Griselda, the post is no sinecure."

"Now for propriety," exclaimed Grisel, starting
to her feet, and seating herself demurely in a
large arm-chair. "I hear Aunt Griselda's voice,
and she cannot bear to see me sitting on the floor."

"Not a very grievous offence, surely, after all,"
replied Jack.

"It is only a posture for tailors, my dear,"
whispered Grisel, mimicking her aunt's tone and
manner.

But there was time for no more, as Miss

Romney entered the room, resplendent in black silk and sable.

"My dear Grisel," she exclaimed, "why did you not ring for tea? I was obliged to go out, Mr. Hunt, and never doubted but that I had left you in good hands!"

"I am very sorry, Aunt Griselda. I quite forgot about tea."

"Never mind, Miss Romney," said Jack in the same breath. "I must take the blame on my own shoulders, by occupying your niece's attention so completely."

"I am most distressed. You will have to improve your memory, Grisel, or you will never make a good housekeeper."

Miss Romney's hospitality was her tenderest point. Her urbanity was rarely so discomposed; but Jack's protestations, that he rarely took tea, and Grisel's evident distress, at last tranquillised her. She gave them a minute history of all she had seen and done, and then retired to see if Miss Romney proper wanted anything.

"I must go also, Grisette; I have some work to do this evening. Unless I get through my writing now, I shall be unable to take a holiday a few weeks later."

"You will remember to go and see Lady Meredith? She will think I have forgotten to deliver her message if you do not," answered Grisel.

"Well, to save your reputation I may go, some day; but I cannot promise for certain."

"Oh, that's equal to a promise, I consider; and, besides, you *must* go to please me."

CHAPTER IV.

AFTER FOUR YEARS.

WHEN Grisel proposed to Jack that their marriage should be within the next few months, it was the end of February. It was now the beginning of April, and Easter was over. The gay world was resuming its festivities, and with the commencement of the season the Romneys had returned to the Manor. Philip Jerningham was in Yorkshire with the Wylds, making arrangements for the future. Augusta was also there. She and Philip were to be at the Manor some weeks later, and Jack was to take a week's holiday at the same time. So, in the meanwhile, Grisel was devoting her energies to learning housekeeping, that she might be quite free to enjoy herself when they were all together. Reggie Mainwaring was expected home about May, and Grisel was delighted that he would arrive in time for her wedding.

To return to London. Jack was, as usual, working hard. The gay doings in the metropolis had no enticements to offer him; he had never even fulfilled his half promise to Grisel, to renew his acquaintance with Lenore Meredith. He had by no means forgotten it, but he put off the visit from day to day.

He had seen Lenore twice. Once, as he passed her house, he caught sight of her at the window, and another time, as her carriage waited at the door of her husband's club. He was close to her the second time, but she did not see him, as she was engaged in conversation with some lady friend.

At last one day he met Lord Meredith, who accosted him warmly, and congratulated him on his marriage. "Lady Meredith has been expecting to see you for some weeks."

Jack pleaded business as his excuse, but had to promise to go and see Lady Meredith the following day.

He did not call till late in the afternoon. He half hoped that he would find Lenore was not alone; the awkwardness of the first meeting would be considerably lessened if it were not *tête-à-tête.*

Lord Meredith had forgotten to tell his wife of his meeting with Jack Hunt. She was lying on the sofa when he entered the room; her solitary afternoons were so rarely disturbed that she had not expected visitors.

The Merediths had kept their return home a secret from the general world; they did not wish it known, at any rate until Lenore was more able for society.

And certainly the weather was not such as to tempt the public out of doors. Steady rain had fallen all day, and none but those compelled by business were abroad.

Lenore's sofa was near the window, and she was lying watching the rain, as it splashed unceasingly into the puddles. There was a fascination in it; and, besides, it had grown too dark for reading. The lamplighter was going his rounds, and a barrel organ was grinding under the window "The Last Rose of Summer" at twice its ordinary pace. The yellow light from the lamps served only to illumine the dripping umbrellas of hurrying foot passengers.

Within the room the fire blazed cheerily, and

Lenore, turning from the glistening picture outside
to the rich comfort of the room, was conscious
of the pleasure she felt in a settled home. She
was expecting the young lord for his half-hour
before dinner; she looked round with a smile
as a hand was laid on the door, but it was not
the child, and she· hurriedly rose as Mr. Hunt's
name was announced.

It was a painful moment for both of them,
though, outwardly, Lenore was the more composed
of the two.

Four years ago they parted as lovers, with all
the passionate pain of disappointed hope within
them ; now they must meet as mere acquaintance
—a cold touch of the hand, and that was
all.

Lenore had risen to her feet as Jack entered
the room. "You have come at last," she said.

"At last, Lady Meredith, and I am grieved to
find you in such delicate health. I hoped, as you
had ventured to return to this perfect climate of
ours, you had in some measure recovered your
strength."

"I am ashamed that you should find me on
the sofa, but, believe me, it is not my custom.
I am rather more tired than usual to-day, having

been out in the rain this afternoon doing some necessary shopping. That's all."

"When did you return from the Continent?" he asked. "Have you been long in town?"

"No, not long, not quite two months yet, and we are only to be here a little longer. We are going to our place in ——shire early in summer. From Lord Meredith's wanderings, the house required some amount of repair; but we kept our return here a secret. We did not wish to be inundated with strangers."

"You must blame Lord Meredith for my visit. It was he who sent me here to-day," Jack answered.

"He knew what my wishes were, and acted accordingly," said Lenore. "But enough about self. I must congratulate you, Mr. Hunt, very much indeed, on your approaching marriage. Mr. Jerningham introduced Miss Romney to me, and she was good enough to come and see me several times before she left town. I have quite lost my heart to her; she is very charming."

"She is a great deal more so than I deserve," said Jack, and then came an awkward pause; it seemed so impossible to ignore the past.

Lenore made an effort to break the uncomfortable silence.

"What are you doing now?" she asked. "Miss Romney said you were working too hard; she was distressed about it."

"Oh, I am all right. I have long ago come to the conclusion that the only safeguard for man is work."

"Safeguard from what?"

"Safeguard from self, and from the tormenting powers of one's own thoughts."

"Have you still the old dread of self?" Lenore asked very earnestly. She had for the moment quite forgotten the events which had passed since the days at The Hurst. There was something in Jack which had always elicited her strongest sympathies. He was in one of his cynical moods, she felt. Had she still the power to dispel it? Surely she need not forego her friendship, because it could never be anything more.

"Do you remember, years ago," she continued, "when I first knew you at Hurst, you asked me how I could love my solitary walks? Then there was nothing you dreaded more than facing your own identity. Is it still the same?"

"Something like it," he answered. "I remember every word you said that night. You spoke of religion being a saving power; you spoke of faith as the rope between heaven and earth. What you said influenced me at the time. Since then, I have grown to think that, though it may be very well for some mortals, still, after all, it is an unsatisfying creed. Faith is a plant difficult of culture in this nineteenth century. In theory it is well enough, but there is a great deal of sentiment about the whole thing."

"If such are your feelings, no wonder you take refuge in work. All the best years of your life it will be one perpetual cry of work, for you are not a man to drown self in any other way ; and then, when the end comes, what will the work avail ? You will have to face yourself at last."

"Before the end comes, I shall have a sweet saint between me and the Judge. Grisel will keep my conscience for me."

Lenore's words moved him more than he cared to own. His only escape was in apparent heartlessness.

"Do you think you will ever rest contented with that ?" exclaimed Lenore, her voice quivering from suppressed feeling. "Do you ever imagine for a moment that such a division of work will bring you satisfaction ?"

"Why not ? Women do the religion for the

world; or, at least, they take the larger share. Men must work, and women must do the religion!"

"You divide the motto wrong. Man, as well as woman, must both work and pray. Believe me, there is no other way—no middle course."

"Why do you take the trouble to speak so to me, Lenore?" Jack had risen to his feet and paced the room. "You stir up all the old longings for something higher and better than one's daily life."

Her name had escaped his lips unconsciously; it thrilled her through and through, but she said nothing. It could not be wrong to let it pass that once; it was not her fault, and so she remained silent.

He came up to where she was sitting, and leant against the mantelpiece.

"You do not answer me," he said. "Do you still take interest enough in me to care whether I go to the dogs or not?"

"Yes," she answered; "if you will have it so, we may be friends as long as we live."

"If such then may be the case, tell me why it is that you so condemn work; without it, one would go utterly wrong."

"But I do not condemn it. No, a thousand

times no. Thank God for work. How could we ever live without it? Only it is not everything. It is simply what you called it at first, 'a safeguard.' It *must* not be all-engrossing!"

"In fact, the state of the case is," he said, "that where you have missed earthly happiness, you may stop up the gap with work."

"Some one has written," said Lenore, "that there is a higher than happiness for the children of men. They may miss happiness and find blessedness; but work will never bring the latter. It may stop the aching void, it may distract thought for the time; but when at last decay comes on, and mind and body refuse to work, what then?"

"Religion comes so much more naturally to you than to us," he said impatiently; "you seem to imbibe it from your cradles. My mother died when I was born, and those things are usually taught by mothers; my father never spoke on such subjects. I thought I was a credit to myself until I first met you. I had kept free from most of the temptations that surround a young man who is his own master. I was proud of my own strength of purpose. My motive was nothing higher than that to act otherwise would be derogatory to me, Jack Hunt; and then came the time when I first knew you, and your life was a new experience to me. You lived in a higher atmosphere than other women I had met, your life and conduct were framed on a different principle. You attracted me from the first moment I saw you. You awakened in me the knowledge of the want of religion in myself. It was my first cry after better things."

"And then?" exclaimed Lenore, breathlessly.

"And then," he continued, "I thought by incorporating this new life I had found with my own I should gradually grow to her standard. She would be there to point the way. And so I followed up the friendship I had begun, and then——"

"Don't," cried Lenore; "I cannot bear it."

"And then I was going to say you failed me. Now I know, and—— Silence a moment, you must let me speak. Now I know all the story of your marriage, of your father's debt, of the money paid down, of the obligation you were under, only to be repaid in one way, of——"

"I cannot be silent!" exclaimed Lenore. "Remember you speak of my husband. And for all the years of his care and love for me I owe him

E

untold gratitude; and, besides, one could not be the wife of such a man without loving him."

"You couldn't be the woman you are," said Jack, very gently, "without loving him. Do not fear, Lady Meredith; you may listen gladly to all I would say of your husband."

"Go on, please; tell me the rest of your story."

"I pass over the time which gave us all our joy and pain. It left me," he said, "without much caring what I did in the world. Instead of trusting you, I engaged myself to Grisel Romney. If you would marry, so should I. I did her incalculable wrong in offering love which was not mine to give. I have suffered for it since, for as I would have her love me, she loves me not. You know what she is, Lady Meredith. You know all her sunny brightness. You must have felt it, for she is the same to all. She loves me as a child would love; she has no influence over me as a woman."

"It will come," said Lenore, simply; "you will teach her to love you, and she in return will, as a child only can, teach you true religion."

"If such as I can learn," he answered gravely.

She rose to her feet and stood beside him at the mantelpiece. He noticed how fragile-looking she

had become, though in the excitement of their
talk her face had gained an unwonted colour and
her eyes beamed brightly. She certainly was the
most perfectly beautiful woman he had ever seen.

"Of course you can learn," she said. "You
must promise me that you will not return to your
work as your one absorbing interest. You have
true, pure, human happiness lying for you in the
future ; and then Grisel will teach you the higher
life."

" I would promise you anything, Lady Meredith."

They were both standing with their back to the
door ; they did not perceive that it had opened,
and that Lord Meredith was in the room. He
overheard Jack's last remark, and for a moment he
glanced from one to the other. He noticed the
sparkle in his wife's eyes ; he noted also the
intense earnestness with which Jack was speaking.
He had time for no more. Lenore had seen him
reflected in a mirror, and turned gladly to meet
him.

"Here is Mr. Hunt, Fred," she said. "We have
been having a long firelight talk, and I have been
making him promise not to work so hard." Lenore,
as she turned, had caught the look of questioning
wonder on her husband's face. She would set

his mind at rest at once. "Miss Romney," she
continued, "was quite unhappy about it when I
saw her; so, as an old friend, I was giving him
good advice."

"She keeps everyone in order that she comes
near, Hunt. I hope you will profit by her
admonitions."

Lord Meredith was ashamed of even his
momentary wonder; he was more cordial than
usual, if possible, in consequence.

"Lenore, you are looking tired," he said at last,
after they had relapsed for some time into general
conversation. "You have not been doing too
much, have you, child?"

"I think I caught a little cold when I was out,"
she said. "I am shivering, and my head aches.
I am going to send Mr. Hunt away for to-day."

"You will send him with me to the smoking
room. Hunt, we have time for a cigar before
dinner."

"Thank you; I shall be very glad. I hope I
have not tired you really," he said, turning to
Lenore.

"Not at all. And you will come and see me
very soon again? I shall be so anxious to hear
about you and your work."

So he and her husband left, and she went to her own room to rest her aching head. The child came to her there, but she could not bear his laughing prattle long. He was dismissed again to the nursery.

That night about eleven Lord Meredith sent for the doctor, and next morning Lenore was worse.

CHAPTER V.

IN TIME FOR THE WEDDING.

"THERE is no doubt about it that Grisel Romney is the very last woman in the world I should ever have guessed as likely to have attracted Jack Hunt. It is simply unintelligible to me."

The speaker was Miss Jerningham; the person addressed, Mrs. Wyld. They were together in the library at The Hurst, Augusta equipped for travelling. She was just starting for Romney Manor, and was giving Mrs. Wyld a piece of her mind before so doing.

"I have never seen Miss Romney, but she seems very charming from description," Mrs. Wyld answered; "and Mr. Hunt is such a favourite of mine, I must believe that anyone he cares for enough to marry must be nice."

"Oh! you are always so anxious to prove everyone is nice. I suppose it is some fault in my composition, but I find the reverse is much easier to prove. I dare say you think me a well-developed specimen of uncharitableness."

Augusta spoke with suppressed self-satisfaction. If she had had the re-composition of herself, she would certainly not have omitted the fault that she confessed. It was to her a great blot in Mrs. Wyld's character, a certain proneness to leniency of judgment.

"You see I go on my husband's principle," Mrs. Wyld answered good-humouredly. "He always says it is better to begin with a fair judgment of everyone. You may be mistaken, but the mistake is easily rectified, as the world is quite willing at a moment's notice to forget everything good it has heard; but it is almost impossible to remove the impression made by an unjust judgment."

"It is a pity that I have not a husband also; I might have come more up to your standard of charity. However, one thing is quite evident: Mr. Hunt cannot be very far gone. Don't tell me that a man really in love would wait four years without any reason for doing so."

"There may be a reason, though the public are

not made aware of the fact," suggested Mrs.
Wyld.

"The public? Yes. But I hardly consider
myself the public. Of course, Phil knows everything, and it is not likely he would leave me in
ignorance. But I shall be able now to form my
own opinion, and I am usually right."

"The marriage is to be immediately, is it not?
You will come in for all the gay doings."

"They say it is to be in June; but I won't
believe it till I see the whole thing done. Jack
Hunt is not married yet, and 'there's many a
slip' you know as well as I do."

Augusta gave a final tug to her dogskin gloves,
and surveyed her travelling costume complacently
in the opposite mirror.

Mrs. Wyld smiled.

"Well, I lay on you as a parting injunction
not to be so candid in the expression of your
opinion at Romney Manor. Least said soonest
mended."

"Your husband says, I suppose," laughed
Augusta. "I must be off, or I shall be late."

Mrs. Wyld accompanied her to the station.

"Remember, I am going to write you a good,
gossiping letter very soon. If I am to be so very

strait-laced at the Manor, I shall certainly require a safety valve somewhere."

Such was Augusta's parting speech.

The Romneys had returned from town some three weeks previously. They were enjoying all the freshness of the glorious spring weather, and Grisel was giving her whole attention to house-keeping. She went about the house in the morning with an anxious face and a large bunch of keys, and Mr. Romney laughed and called her Martha ; but she was too thoroughly in earnest to be turned from her duty by any of the home teasings ; Bryde and Tom certainly gave her little peace, and her father was very nearly as bad.

Grisel had been busy all day. Sybil declared she had never had so much time to herself before, her sister did everything ; and as Bryde said she would not deprive Grisette of the pleasure of being useful for the world, the latter became an important personage in the household. It was late in the afternoon. Bryde and Philip had gone to meet Augusta, and the home party were expecting their return immediately.

Sybil and Grisel were together ; Lady Main-waring had driven over after lunch, and had just left.

"I am thankful Sir Roger is better; it would have been such a sad home-coming for Reggie had it been otherwise."

Sybil was the speaker, and Grisel, with her back turned towards her sister, was watching the road by which the party from the station would return.

"I wonder when he will arrive? Lady Main-waring said to-night or to-morrow. Oh, I am longing to see him!"

"You will be quite overpowered, Grisette, with happiness. Have you forgotten Jack is also coming in a day or two?"

"No, that I haven't—dear old Jack—but of course I have seen him quite recently, and it is four years since I said good-bye to Reggie. I almost hope Jack will not come till after Le Gris has arrived. I should like to have him all to myself just at first."

The door opened to admit Bryde and the Jerninghams.

"Why, Grisel," exclaimed Augusta, "you have missed us by gazing from the wrong window. I thought a young lady in your situation would only have taken her seat at the window to watch for one loved form."

Grisel jumped up to welcome her guest. Her face had flushed under Augusta's keen inspection.

"Mr. Hunt is in town," she said, quietly. "No amount of watching would have brought him; and, besides, I surely may watch for my sister and friends."

"Never mind, Grisette," said Philip; "it is quite evident Augusta has never been in your situation. When she is booked for some one, she will understand that it becomes *ennuyant* at times to fill your mind with one idea. It is quite possible to have too much of a good thing."

"We passed Lady Mainwaring," remarked Bryde. "Has she been here?"

"Yes; she came to tell us that Reggie is expected either to-night or to-morrow," Sybil said. "Sir Roger is better, so she was in good spirits."

"As soon as that? I shall be very glad to see Reggie again—very glad indeed."

"I do not suppose you are singular in your sentiments, Miss Bridget; eh, Grisel?"

Philip was in a teasing mood. Augusta followed her brother's eyes, and saw the colour mount to Grisel's face.

"I certainly am glad to see him, Phil. I see no harm in it."

"Oh, no; none in the least. Only, I say I am sorry for poor Jack."

"You live in a chronic state of sorrow for Jack. May I tell him so? I am going to write to him before dinner, and tell him that Sir Roger is better and Reggie coming home."

"What order he has you in, Grisette! Are you obliged to confess to him in every letter? If so, I advise you to write without fail this evening. It would be better in every respect."

Grisel was leaving the room when Philip uttered the last speech. She turned a laughing face to him. "Why?" she asked; "it seems to me that to-morrow would do just as well."

"It might do as well, if there are no new arrivals before then; but you see there is a chance of some one coming to-night, and if you write to-night, then you need not do so again for a day or two. By that time the joy of meeting will have partially subsided, and your letter to the absent will have acquired a healthier tone. Do you comprehend, my dear Griselda?"

Again Augusta noted the crimson deepen on Grisel's cheek.

"What nonsense you talk, Philip," she said, and left the room. Silence fell on those left behind, and then Sybil broke the awkward pause by asking if Augusta would like to go to her room?

Augusta had made several notes during the last half-hour. Her letter to Mrs. Wyld would certainly be an entertaining one. She had come to the Manor resolved to solve the mystery of that four years' engagement. She thought she was already on the right track.

The morning sun shone straight in at Grisel's bedroom window. She woke with a start—was it late? She had to gather flowers before breakfast, so there was no time to lose.

It was difficult to dress quickly on such a morning. Through the trellis of branches and of clustering roses that framed her window she looked out over miles of rolling country. The house stood on rising ground, and over the tops of the beechwood she saw the river winding a silver streak among the fields till it lost itself in the woods of Bramleigh Hall. Grisel's thoughts followed the river, and were lost in the woods also. Pleasant thoughts they must have been, for, instead of coiling up her golden hair, she pushed the curls from her temples and stood at the open window thinking. The smiles gathered round her lips, and her eyes grew soft and wistful as she gazed. Then slowly and sedately the clock at the stables struck eight. She turned from the window and finished her toilette. She slipped her pearl hoop on her finger.

"Dear old Jack," she said, "I hope he is not working too hard;" and then she gave her canary some fresh seed and water, and putting on her shady hat she ran down to the garden.

Flitting from flower to flower, filling her basket with choicest blossoms, singing gaily to herself all the time, she seemed the fairest flower of all to Reggie Mainwaring, as he stood and watched her in silent admiration. He dare hardly break the delight of the moment by announcing his presence. Having arrived late the evening before, he had come to see the Romneys. The breakfast hour was a late one at Bramleigh Hall; he would have time for a glimpse of them all, and yet be back before his mother missed him.

So Grisel gathered her flowers unconscious of his gaze.

But her basket was filled at last, and then, before returning to the house, she turned to give

one final look at the perfect loveliness of the
May morning.

"This time next year I shall be in London," she
thought, with a little sigh. "How I shall miss
the country! Dear me, the time is coming so
near now—only one more month to enjoy it all;
but there is one comfort after all, that Jack won't
be so dull when I am there to look after him.
But oh! I wish I could take them all with me—
Papa, and Sybil, and Bryde, and Tom; then I
shouldn't mind half so much."

It seemed to Reggie that there had come into
her face a trace of some vague, undefined yearning
after something she had not. Perhaps it was but
a shadow of a summer cloud. Perhaps it was
mere fancy, a reading of his own thoughts reflected
in her face. It did not last a moment—had it
ever been there, he could hardly tell; but as her
eyes wandered over the landscape, she espied him,
and then came such a look of glad surprise. He
stepped from his hiding-place, and clasped her
hands.

"La Grise, my queen!" he exclaimed.

"Le Gris, you have come at last. I have missed
you so." She raised her eyes to his as frankly
as in the old days, but suddenly her eyelids

dropped, and an entirely new sensation of shyness
came over her.

"Let us go into the house, Reggie; the others
will wish to see you also."

"There is no hurry, La Grise. Wait a few
minutes, and tell me all about yourself and the
others."

"There is not much to tell," she said. "You
know all about Philip and Bryde. Phil's sister is
here just now. I am a little bit afraid of her.
Then Papa and Tom and Sybil are just the
same as usual. That is all, I think, except
myself."

"And yourself?"

"I am to be married this day month, Le Gris.
I don't quite understand it yet, but I dare say I
shall in time. And Jack has been working too
hard; so you see it must be soon, so that I can
take care of him."

"Is he here also, La Grise?"

"No; he is coming in a day or two, and then
you must get very good friends with him, so that
after we are married you can come and stay with
us. Then you will see how much I have improved
since you left. I have tried so hard to learn all
a woman ought to know."

"Why, La Grise," Reggie interrupted, "you told me once that girls did not become women until they were thirty, and you are a long way from that yet."

"So I thought in the old days, Le Gris; but then, you know, it never entered my head that I should be married so soon, and that of course alters things entirely."

"Yes, entirely," thought Reggie to himself, but he only said, "So I have come home in time to dance at your wedding, Grisette!"

"We'll not talk of that just now," she answered. "Let us go into the dining-room. They will be so surprised to see you here."

So the two went together up the pathway, and disappeared from Miss Jerningham's sight.

She had had an interesting half-hour. Early rising was one of the points she prided herself on. She preached it also to her brother, but Philip did not see it, usually coming into the room as everyone had finished breakfast. This morning Augusta had been amply rewarded for her self-denial. Her window overlooked the garden, and immediately Grisel appeared, she said within herself it was for some reason.

So now, having seen the meeting, she felt

F

certain she was right. She knew Reggie Mainwaring perfectly by description.

She closed her book of morning meditations
that lay open before her, as the gong for breakfast
sounded. She had but a dim idea of what she
had read.

When she entered the dining-room, she was
taken utterly aback to find a stranger added to
the family party.

CHAPTER VI.

EDGED TOOLS.

IT was after breakfast the following day. Grisel and Augusta were alone together; the post had just come in, and the former retired into the window-seat to enjoy a letter she had just received from Jack. Augusta's correspondence was of a more voluminous character; it was some time before she could turn her attention to her companion.

Jack's letter did not contain much; he told Grisel of his daily life, and of how much he looked forward to seeing her the following day; a few words at the end were given to saying how bright his future looked now in comparison to what it did a few weeks ago. "You will have your hands full, little Grisel," he wrote; "you will have to teach me many things which none but your own sweet self can teach. Are you afraid of the bargain you have made, Grisette ? Shall I say you may go free ? No, child, I am too selfish for that. I have not long to wait now, and as the time draws near," &c., &c.

Such effusions are only readable by lovers ; for the general public there is apt to be monotony in the subject.

Grisel read it twice all through, folded it, and put it in her pocket. She clasped her hands on her knees and looked out of the window. She was trying to understand it all. Instead of pleasure, her lover's assurances seemed to fill her with lurking fears. What had she done that he should love her so? What did he expect of her that made him count the hours of the next few weeks ? And, after all, if he should find himself mistaken, if he should be disappointed in her !

Augusta had finished the perusal of her letters. She let them lie on her knee. She was silently watching Grisel, trying to read the thoughts that were passing through her mind.

"Not bad news, I hope, Grisel ?" she said, at last.

"No ; not at all bad news. Was I looking grave ? I was only dreaming."

"And they were not pleasant dreams, I fear. Mr. Hunt, I hope, is not going to prove false?"

"Oh, no; he is coming to-morrow. How long is it since you have seen him, Miss Jerningham?" she asked.

"More than four years. The last time we met we were in the same house together, or rather he spent most of the day with us. We were a more attractive party there than that at the house where he was really staying. We were all at The Hurst. I'll tell you who was there—a handsome Miss Fenton and her father. By-the-bye, I hear, in one of my letters to-day, that she is very ill. She married Lord Meredith, you know."

"So that was where Jack met Lady Meredith," exclaimed Grisel, brightening into interest. "I knew that they were old friends, but I never knew how they first came to know each other."

"Mr. Hunt told you that they were old friends, did he?" laughed Augusta. "Well, I suppose he spoke the truth."

"What do you mean?" asked Grisel. "Why should it not be true, and why should he not have told me?"

"Oh, I mean nothing; only I wondered that you had never heard that in the old days Lenore

Fenton and Mr. Hunt were more than ordinarily
good friends!"

"I do not wonder at it," said Grisel, simply.
"I told Mr. Hunt one day that I wondered he
had not fallen in love with Lady Meredith.
I certainly should have done so had I been he."

"And Mr. Hunt answered, of course, that you
were the first and only woman he had ever
loved?"

"I see no 'of course' about the matter, Miss
Jerningham. If Mr. Hunt had said so, I should
not have believed him. You know a man never
marries his first love."

"Nor a woman either, Grisel; *you* know that,
of course." Augusta's eyes watched closely for
the tell-tale blush which she felt sure must come,
but she was disappointed.

"There are exceptions to every rule, Miss
Jerningham," said Grisel, haughtily, as she left
the room.

Grisel believed Augusta spoke in a general way.
She never for a moment entertained the idea that
it could be anyone in particular to whom she
alluded; so her manner was as unconstrained as
usual when Reggie came in the afternoon.

She had promised to go on the river with him.

Unless she went that day she would not go at all, he thought; she would have a prior claim on her time to-morrow.

He never paused to consider the wisdom of his actions. It could do Grisel no harm. Was she not to be married within the month? and for himself the temptation was too strong to be resisted.

So, after a lapse of years, they found themselves once more on the river. Nothing around changed since the day that Reggie had rowed Grisel up to the island the night before she went to school. The woods and ferns were then, as now, in all the freshness of early summer; the weather was as gloriously bright. Grisel was not seventeen then, and wore short dresses; now, she was twenty-one, and wore long ones — that was about all the change in her. He was also five years older, and all those five years his love for Grisel had undergone no change, save strengthened with his strength. He believed it was an utterly hopeless love; he would have knocked anyone down who dared to suggest the possibility of its being otherwise. With such feelings it was perfectly safe to renew old days. He was the only one who would suffer for it; and if he were willing to take this extra burden on himself, who was there in the wide world who had any right to stop him? Certainly there was no one, and humanity has not yet learnt to refrain from these self-imposed burdens.

Yet, somehow, that afternoon it was very hard not to speak of his love. Floating idly down the stream, with the lulling sound of the water lapping on the sides of the boat, everything glowing with sunshine; Nature herself was giving him an intoxicating cup; and then, added to all, Grisel was in a dreamy mood, lolling in the stern of the boat, enjoying to the full the *dolce far niente* existence.

She looked up at last after some time of silence. "Isn't it perfect, Reggie?" she said. "I do not know how I shall ever live without our river. Ever since we were quite little, you and I have always been together boating, and I know I shall miss it terribly."

"I do not think you will, Grisette. Your happiness lies in the future. Very soon you will have forgotten all about these afternoons, or remember them only as an incident in your childhood."

"My happiness will have to be very overwhelming before it will make me forget the past. Does marriage really necessitate the forgetting of all the old pleasures and friends ?"

" It is not an unlikely case," he answered. " By degrees other interests will creep into your life. You will come to the Manor now and then. Perhaps we may meet, perhaps not, who knows ? And there may even come a time when you will hear my name mentioned, and you will remember that we once knew each other."

" I wonder," she answered, dreamily, " if you are saying all this because you feel that such a time is coming for you. You will marry some day."

" That I never shall do," he interrupted, earnestly.

She went on as if she had not heard his words.

" You will marry, and then interests will creep into *your* life, and *you* will forget all about us ; or, perhaps, you may see by the newspapers that one of us—that, perhaps, I am dead—and then *you* will remember that we once knew each other !"

" I shall have nothing to make me forget," he said.

" Neither shall I. I must ever look back to these days all my life through ; and Reggie, do you know, I shall grow to be sorry that you came back from India if we are both to forget all about it. I never knew how much I had missed it all till you came home, till I saw you in the garden yesterday. Whether you do or not, I shall always remember how happy we have been."

If Grisel had betrayed the slightest consciousness or shyness in what she said, Reggie would have told her then and there how unlikely he was ever to forget; but she spoke so simply about it all, that he remained silent. What use was there in telling her of a hopeless love?

"It is very unfortunate that you are not my brother," she said at length, "and then all those gloomy forebodings of forgetting each other would be impossible. It never enters my head to tell Tom that soon we shall have other interests, &c., &c., and so we may as well make up our minds to the inevitable; and yet, Le Gris, until now I have seen as much, in fact, almost more of you than of Tom. It is such an odd world, I cannot understand it at all. Now, don't you agree with me in wishing that you were my brother?"

"If it would give you any satisfaction, Grisette, yes; but, somehow, I hardly think it would have been——"

He stopped short suddenly. "Second thoughts are best," he said, and turned the conversation.

Then they talked of many things — reminiscences of long ago, of many a day spent together, many a scrape in which they had shielded each other. Grisel's laughter rang over the water at the quaint recollections of their childhood.

The rest of the party heard it as they wandered through the woods at the river-side.

"Grisette is as much a child as ever," said Sybil; "she and Reggie had always some private joke going on."

"And Grisel delights in fun," interposed Bryde.

"That is unfortunate," said Augusta, drily, "as I hear that Mr. Hunt is rarely seen to laugh or smile. She is wise to make the most of her opportunities."

"It's on the old principle that 'extremes meet,'" said Philip, who was one of the party. "But Jack's gravity is a new phase in his existence. He used to be as merry as possible; Grisel will soon teach him to laugh again."

"I don't remember that he was so easily amused," Augusta answered her brother. "I am sure at Hurst, when he did laugh, it was usually at one, not with one."

"I suppose you fell a victim, or your memory would not be so good," said Philip, and the party disappeared in the woods.

Meanwhile, Reggie and Grisel, never dreaming that their merriment was subject for animadversion, continued unheeding.

Reggie finished some anecdote; it served to remind Grisel of another.

"Oh, do you remember that dreadful day, Le Gris, when we dropped your mother's watch down the grating in the old cellar?"

"Yes," said Reggie, laughing, "and we tried to hook it up again with a crooked pin at the end of a string."

"How was it that you dropped it, Reggie? I wasn't there, you know. Bryde was with you, and when you failed you came to me."

"Because your hands were so small, and neither Bryde nor I could get ours through the grating. My mother had let me have her watch whilst I learnt my lessons, and Bryde came in suddenly with the news that the rabbits had escaped into the old cellar. Of course, I never thought about the watch, for my father had only let me have the rabbits on condition that they were never to be allowed to go loose."

"Dear me," said Grisel, "what a time ago it seems, and yet how well I remember how thoroughly miserable you and Bryde looked when you came for me."

"We should have been in a bad way, La Grise, had it not been for you. I never saw such small hands; but even for them it was wonderful how they ever got through the grating."

"It was rather painful work, certainly," said Grisel, rubbing her hand at the remembrance.

"I don't think they have grown at all since then," he said.

She laughed, and pulled off one of her rings, tossing it to him.

"Try if you can get it on, Le Gris; it is far too large for me."

But the ring would not go on, and he returned it to its owner.

"Mine, I believe, would nearly fit your wrist," he said, and drew it off."

"Do take care, Reggie, and do not drop it; it is such a perfect beauty, far too good for a man. I have been watching it flash in the sunlight, and admiring it so."

Grisel slipped the ring on every finger in turn.

"I believe it would fit this finger best. Look

now, and admire it, please.   Does it not look
well ?"

She had taken off her engagement ring, and
put it on her third finger, and held out her
hand for his inspection.

"Don't you admire it, Reggie ?   I think it is
perfect."

She looked into his face to read his thoughts,
and he already was looking at her.

"Why don't you admire it, Le Gris ?" she said,
hurriedly.   Her eyes had dropped before his gaze.
She had read something in his look which she
had never understood before—a something which
made her pulses throb, and a strange tightening
came in her throat.

Reggie turned suddenly away ; for a moment
only had he forgotten himself.   When he looked
again, she had taken his ring from her finger.
He spoke then in his usual way.

"I wish you to keep the ring, Grisel.   It is
my wedding present to you.   It is, as you say,
too good for a man, so you must accept it to
please me."

"Oh, Le Gris, I couldn't think of taking it.
It is far too good for me, and, besides, it is too
large."

"That is a fault easily rectified; and I would rather see it on your hands than anywhere else, my queen."

So, after a little more argument, she accepted her wedding present, and sat admiring it with childish delight—a single diamond in a band of gold.

"It is my first diamond ring, and, Reggie, I am so glad you gave it to me."

She had forgotten all about her momentary confusion in the pleasure of the gift.

The afternoon was wearing on, and the sun was casting long shadows as once more they neared home. Reluctantly Reggie steered the boat to the shore, and, alighting, turned to assist Grisel. Suddenly there came to Grisel's mind a remembrance of the past; she had forgotten it all through those years. Something in the surroundings brought the scene back to her now. Reggie had then taken her bundle of ferns from her, and, in doing so, had kissed her hand. Her heart gave a throb; for a moment she dreaded he might be guilty of the same offence. Before he could stop her, she had leaped ashore.

"You have no ferns in your hands to-night, La Grise," he said.

She was right; he had remembered it also, and she turned her head away.

She was thankful that at that moment the rest of the party emerged from the wood. They had been following the course of the river also, though they had lost sight of those in the boat; but as they neared the pier, Augusta exclaimed—

"There are Mr. Mainwaring and Grisel. Let us join them."

They all walked up to the house together. Mr. Romney met them as they entered the garden.

"Papa," exclaimed Grisel, running forward, "look at what Le Gris has given me. Is it not beautiful? It is my wedding present."

Mr. Romney was not the only one to admire.

"It is not new," was all Reggie said.

And Augusta made another mental note.

CHAPTER VII.

A HARD TRUTH.

AND all those bright weeks of spring, ever since the day she had seen Jack Hunt, Lenore Meredith had been ill. Nothing very dangerous at first—a low, lingering typhoid fever, one day better, the next worse.

Many and constant were the inquiries made by anxious friends, but the answer was always the same. There was nothing new to tell; the physicians were not alarmed, but anxious, at the steady persistence of the fever. Her illness could not be traced to any very definite cause; it began with the chill caught the day she was out in the rain. That was four weeks ago, and she had so little strength at the beginning that it was now reduced in a very great degree.

She was not the least anxious about herself,

G

but full of concern for all those around her. She
would not rest until Lord Meredith consented to
be some hours a-day away from her sick-room,
nor would she let him be disturbed by night-
watching; and even after he had agreed to her
terms, her mind was constantly on the alert,
planning and thinking of things for his comfort,
that he might the less feel her absence.

Then her boy usurped her attention. Towards
night she would get restless and excited, thinking
that everything was not going on as usual.
Perhaps she heard the child cry, and would fret
herself that he was missing her; or at other times,
with the unreasoning fancies of fever, his very
silence would create cause of alarm. On several
occasions she had been delirious, but these times
had never as yet lasted long, and they fondly
hoped that the worst of the fever was past.

For a few days there were certainly symptoms
to justify such hopes, but the weather suddenly
grew very mild for the time of the year—hot,
steamy days towards the end of May. Farmers
in the country were rejoicing in it for their crops,
but in the metropolis one longed for even the

freshness of the March winds. It was enervating, exhausting even to those in health, and the nurse saw with anxiety how her patient suffered from it.

It was towards evening. The day had been even warmer than the preceding ones, and in consequence Lenore was much excited, and rambling a good deal in her talk. When the doctor came for his afternoon visit she did not know him, though her light-headedness passed off soon, and on her husband entering the room shortly afterwards, she was quite herself again.

She asked him what he had been doing, and instead of dismissing him at once, she begged him to stay beside her. He took his book and remained in the room, sending the nurse out to walk. Lenore was less restless, and when he went down to his eight o'clock dinner, he thought she seemed rather better.

Later in the evening he was with her again; he was going to watch the first half of the night, and the nurse had gone to bed. Lady Meredith's maid was in the adjoining room, but he preferred being alone with Lenore. She had fallen asleep, and in the quiet he had time to note the ravages fever had committed. All her long hair had been cut short, and the small clustering curls which were left made her look singularly young and girlish. Her hands had grown so thin, that her wedding-ring was in danger of slipping off. A cold chill ran through him as he noted it all. What if he were about to lose her? Their happiness had been so complete, so ideal, it might be that it was too bright to last. Nothing had ever come between them, not a word had disturbed their peace. He felt that she understood him so entirely, he had hardly a thought which he did not share with her. He had told her of his past life, his love for her mother, and she knew well his love for herself; and of her past life he knew nothing. It had occurred to him once or twice how seldom Lenore spoke of her father.. He had known Sir James well. He supposed that she had found it hard at times to deal with her father's temper; this perhaps was sufficient reason to bury the past under her present happiness. When he knew her first, she was only a girl; nothing had come to break the sunny brightness of her existence.

Lenore moved restlessly in her sleep, the heat oppressed her so. She suddenly awoke with a start, begging to have the window opened. He did what she asked. She appeared satisfied, and lay down again.

So passed an hour. It was nearly midnight, and the air was becoming more close and stifling. Then, in the silence, a low growl of thunder was heard. Soon after, a flash of lightning glanced on the mirror, followed by a nearer peal of thunder.

Lenore moaned, and her husband rose and drew the curtains more closely across the window. There was a pause in the storm, he almost hoped it was passing over, when suddenly the heavens were torn directly above them with one of those sharp, rattling peals as of musketry.

Lenore started up in bed, looking wildly round.

"What was that noise?" she cried. "It wasn't my father's fall? Oh, what was it, Fred? You know I mistook my father's fall for the noise made by the Romneys' boxes; they arrived at the same time. But of course you do not understand; you think I am talking nonsense; you know nothing of my past life!" With that she broke into a jarring laugh.

Lord Meredith was beside her in a moment; he pacified her by degrees, and got her to lie down again. She continued murmuring to herself, but he did not catch her words. Presently, however, the thunder again alarmed her. She clung wildly to her husband's arm, exclaiming—

"Oh, Father, you cannot mean what you say; you cannot mean that I am to give up the man I love, and marry the man that I do not care whether I ever see again? Remember I am a woman, and in love!"

"Be still, my darling, you are at home; no one will make you do what you do not wish!"

She seemed to comprehend the purport of his words.

"But you said I must marry him; you said I would bring dishonour on you if I did not accept Lord Meredith. Did you say that I was to be sold to pay your debts—I, your only child? Father, I cannot do it. I told Jack I would marry him. I love him so, I cannot give him up; I will not do it!" She almost screamed, trying to break away from her husband's hold.

His face had grown véry white and still, and his voice was hard and forced as he said, " My darling, you must be quiet ; you will make yourself worse!"

" I don't care! Cannot I die as well as my father? Did you say I was worse?" she continued, muttering to herself, "Worse, am I? That is well; I shall soon be dead also!"

The perspiration stood on Lord Meredith's brow in cold, bead-like drops, wrung from him in this hour of agony.

"Good God!" he exclaimed, under his breath, "does she hate me so? What have I done to deserve this?"

She was quiet for a moment, but it did not last ; each peal of echoing thunder seemed to arouse her afresh to a renewed sense of her wrong.

She now broke out into a low and mirthful laugh, and began singing, " I love my love, I love my love, because I know my love loves me!" Over and over again came the refrain, while peals of low laughter broke from her.

"And who is my love?" she continued, in hurried accents. "Would you like to know? He said he would keep my love so safe, even in eternity. Jack said that. You know who I mean, Fred? Jack Hunt, my lover, my only lover, he told me that, and you knew nothing of it, but you know now. Aren't you glad to know he loved me?" she continued, triumphantly. "No one else was, no one said they were glad; I was all alone, and then I was sold," she said, dropping her voice. "My father sold me. It was not my fault, I could not help it. I would rather have died!"

Her last words sank into a whisper; she had exhausted herself, and fell back upon her pillows. She was quite tranquil now, and appeared to be falling asleep. Lord Meredith slipped his arm from under her head and turned slowly away, his face and whole bearing expressive of the most abject misery. He dropped into a chair beside the bed, and buried his face in his hands.

"She would rather have died!" he repeated again and again. "Rather have died than become my wife, and I—I only wished her happiness. Bear witness to me, O God! that it was her happiness, not my own, I sought. I dreamt she loved me. I was blind, a fool, to imagine for a moment that one so young, so beautiful, so perfect, could care for me in that way—I, double her age. I acted for good, and nothing but harm has come, nothing but misery for us both. Did I love her too well? Will she die now, leaving me as her parting words that I brought nothing but misery into her life? I, who love her so. I am to go to the grave with this burden on my soul. 'She would rather have died,' she said."

Then came half-an-hour's silence. Lenore lay exhausted, between waking and sleeping; Lord Meredith continued where he was, bowed down with his sorrow.

From time to time she murmured broken sentences, but he could distinguish little of what she said. He heard his own name mentioned, and then repeatedly she appealed to her father.

A hundred questions rose to his mind which he could not answer. Scene after scene presented itself before his mental vision, in which Lenore was present, and when he fondly believed he was all in all to her.

Was all her gentle care and thoughtfulness for him only a part she was acting? Could he have been completely deceived all those years? Must he at once and for ever put away from himself this beautiful dream, and take home the truth that she must ever regard him as the man who had spoilt her life? In future years he must be content to know the love she gave him was wrung from her because of duty, and because the nobility of her nature would never let him feel what she had suffered through no fault of his. And all must be endured in silence; he must never let her know what she herself in her delirium had told him. This was to be his life henceforth. He, too, would have his part to play. Their daily existence must be lived through for the sake of their child; and for him also the sweetness would be gone for ever.

He raised his head from his hands. He could not tell how time had passed, but Lenore had made some movement. She was awake, and lying watching him with large, lustrous eyes. She was quite herself, and smiled as he raised his head.

"Have I been talking in my sleep?" she whispered. "Somehow I think I have been dreaming."

He turned off her question.

"There has been a thunderstorm which made you restless. It is over now, and you must go to sleep again, darling, and awake better to-morrow."

She noticed how worn he looked; the faint light in the room even exaggerated the weary lines on his face.

"Are you very tired, poor old Fred?" she asked. "Were you asleep just now, and I disturbed you? I wonder what I should have done without you all this weary illness. If I get better, it will be entirely owing to your nursing and care."

"You must not speak so, dearest, you will excite yourself. Another would have nursed you even better, perhaps."

"No one could," she whispered. She was so weak she could hardly speak, but her eyes were full of love and gratitude.

If it had only been yesterday, he said to himself,

how her words would have thrilled him.   But now
all was changed.   He turned sadly away, making
an excuse to get something for her.   Could it all
be acting, he asked himself?

But no one heard the mournful question, and
no answer came.

The nurse came in soon after and relieved Lord
Meredith from his watch.   He was very unwilling
to leave the room.   He dreaded a return of the
delirium, and that any ears besides his own should
hear of the gulf which lay between himself and
his wife.

But Lenore, knowing nothing of the cause of
his anxiety, insisted on his leaving her.   She was
too weak to bear the slightest opposition ; the
nurse looked annoyed at even the momentary
hesitation in obeying her ladyship's orders.   Lord
Meredith went to his room with his life's happiness in ashes.

The rest of the night passed quietly, the storm
had spent itself, and the air blew in at the window
cool and fresh.   Lenore slept at intervals.   When
the doctors arrived in the morning, they were
satisfied with their patient ; the fever was entirely

gone. Nothing now remained but the alarming weakness, but Lady Meredith had youth on her side—her recovery might be tedious, but they hoped now it was sure.

It seemed that Lenore steadily gained ground after that one night. She slept a great deal, only awaking to take the constant nourishment that was necessary; she was struggling back slowly to life, and her husband asked himself the awful question, would she rather it had been death?

How ardently he longed to ask herself about it! If he could only hear from her own lips that the skeleton she had raised was but a phantasy of fever! He tried to reason himself into this belief, but he did not succeed; there was ever recurring to his mind the scene which he interrupted the night Lenore was taken ill.

He had been startled at the time, but had forgotten all about it again, until Lenore's confession brought it to his mind. He read it all by a new light now; would to God he had been left in darkness!

All the strangeness of the scene, noted unconsciously at the time, stood before him in unmistakable outline. Coming into the room not more quietly than usual, and yet his wife and Mr. Hunt had been so absorbed in talk they had not noticed him. He had heard the thrill in Lenore's tones as he opened the door, and he was present at Jack's earnest avowal—"I would promise *you* anything, Lady Meredith." Oh! if he could only ask her for an explanation ; but even had it been possible, he dreaded the answer he would receive.

His wife's hearty pleasure at his entrance was hardly consistent with fear ; she had turned to him so naturally, and made him aware of their talk.

He was ashamed of his suspicions, and yet, if she were steadily acting a part, it was only her *rôle* for the time being. His mind was filled with a thousand conflicting ideas ; it was pain of the acutest kind having to doubt the woman he loved, even though he imputed nothing to her but purely unselfish motives. That she still wrongfully loved Jack Hunt never crossed his mind ; it would have been in his eyes a blemish on her unsullied purity that such a thought should even occur to him.

How he had loved her, how he loved her

still, even more alive to the intensity of his passion now than in the days gone by; and how this love had received the cruellest blow that can be given, inflicted by the object beloved, no one would ever know.

Such a wound can hardly be received without some scar being visible. Lenore must have noticed the change in him, had she not been in such a state of weakness that outward objects held but little place in her thoughts. He was there beside her; that was enough for her. She did not observe that her recovery, which would otherwise have been a season of such rejoicing to him, had come, and he still wore the anxious, harassed look that he had carried with him all the time when her danger had been most imminent.

So two or three days passed by. Lenore was gradually gaining ground, and as her strength returned, she was so full of the old love and thoughtfulness about him, that he almost persuaded himself at times that the awful night of the storm must have been some horrid dream— a spectre sent to show that earthly happiness must not be too confident in itself, too sure of duration.

He was sitting beside her one afternoon recounting how he had spent the day, amusing her with tittle and tattle and gossip, when they were interrupted by a servant with the announcement that Mr. Hunt was down stairs, and was most anxious to see his lordship.

Lord Meredith involuntarily glanced at Lenore, but she betrayed not the slightest trace of unusual feeling.

"Do go and see him, Fred ; he will be anxious to know how I am. Tell him I am recovering rapidly, and, if he is going to the Manor, send my love to Grisel Romney."

CHAPTER VIII.

ONLY AN "OLD FRIEND."

"IF I were Mr. Hunt, I should not rest quietly and let my *fiancée* be so continually with another man; it is as well he is coming to-day for all concerned."

"What nonsense you speak, Augusta. Grisel and Reggie Mainwaring have been like brother and sister for years. It would be positively absurd that their acquaintance should cease!"

"Very like brother and sister, certainly. I have not found brothers as a rule in such anxiety to be for ever in their sister's society."

"The feeling may be reciprocal on the part of the sister, Gus. You are not over well pleased

H

to see much of your brother," and Philip proceeded to leave the room.

"Where are you going to now?" exclaimed
Augusta. "Can't you stand my society for five
minutes?"

"I thought it was all the other way," Philip
answered, nonchalantly. "However, I don't mind
listening for a few minutes if you have anything
to say."

He had jumped from the window on to the
grass terrace, and stood leaning on the window-
sill, calmly filling his pipe. He drew his watch
from his pocket. "You can claim my attention
for five minutes; make the most of your time!"
he said.

"Seriously, then, Philip, I think it is quite your
place to say something. Tom is away from home;
you are to be her brother shortly; you can surely
say how unwise you think it — this constant
intimacy. People will not let it pass unnoticed."

"I suppose you pass for 'people;' there are
none others that I am aware of."

"If you will not look on it in that light, surely

you have some interest in Grisel herself. It would be very unpleasant for you if Bryde's sister got into mischief."

"Now we are beginning to see daylight, Gus. Your anxiety is roused by sisterly feelings; but if I tell you that I am not the least alarmed, you can set your mind at rest."

"Really, Philip, you are too provoking. Well, you cannot say you have not been warned if anything disagreeable does occur. If some fine morning Mr. Mainwaring and Grisel are missing, you will not be able to say that you were utterly unprepared for such an *esclandre*."

"Rubbish! What did you eat for supper last night? It has evidently disagreed with you horribly."

"How atrociously rude you are, Philip. There is nothing more to be said, then; as you refuse to speak, I shall."

"Really this is beyond a joke, Augusta. To begin with, you have no business to interfere; and secondly, the whole thing is a creation of your own imagination. Unless you are silent on the subject, I shall be seriously angry. However, I cannot wait any longer now."

"Where are you going, that you are in such a desperate hurry?"

"Bryde, Grisel, Reggie, and I are going on an expedition into the woods. Will you come?"

"No, thank you. Under the circumstances, my company would not be appreciated; besides, I do not approve of the whole thing."

"Oh! if you are going to take the highly injured and moral tone, I dare say you are better at home. There is no necessity to put any force on your inclinations."

Philip turned from the window, and soon Augusta had the satisfaction of seeing the quartette wander down the grass avenue. Their laughter reached her ears; she put down her book impatiently and went to the writing-table. It was a good opportunity for getting over a long letter to Mrs. Wyld.

The above conversation had taken place immediately after lunch. Jack Hunt was to arrive before dinner, and the walking party were to return by the station and escort him to the house. Reggie was spending the day at the Manor; he also was to return for dinner.

Augusta was not left long alone. Presently Sybil entered the room.

"I am going to Langford, our market town. Do you feel inclined for the drive? It is some six miles from here, and the country is very pretty, if you care to see it."

"Thanks; I should like to come. Are you going at once?"

"Yes, if you are ready. The phaeton is to be at the door immediately."

Shortly afterwards the ladies were starting. Mr. Romney stood on the steps giving some final directions to his eldest daughter.

"I thought of returning the other way, Papa, and picking up Jack's portmanteau. It will save us sending for it in the evening."

"Yes, you are right. Only, how do you think that young horse will stand the railway? Remember, you have not tried him yet."

"Oh, he's all right, sir," said the groom.

"The other one is extra quiet, and Miss Romney need 'ave no fear."

They waved an adieu as they disappeared from sight. Sybil's chestnuts were not long in clearing the ground; besides, it would take them all their time to do their commissions and be at the station at the proper hour.

Meanwhile, in the woods the quartette were enjoying themselves immensely. They kept together at first, but after a time they became separated. Philip and Bryde had naturally fallen behind, and Reggie was rejoicing in one more *tête-á-tête* with Grisel.

Gradually the afternoon wore away. The last two mentioned had found a seat among the ferns and moss at the foot of an old tree. They were neither of them in a talkative mood — Reggie because he daren't, and Grisel because she was too perfectly happy to speak. From time to time some commonplace remark passed between them, and then came long, unbroken silences, in which the insects hummed, and the birds sang, and the wind rustled softly amongst the grasses. Away in the distance the river's voice formed a gentle under-current of sound.

Grisel's eyes were bent upon her knee. She was arranging in bunches the wild flowers which she had gathered in her walk, trying the various combinations which they made; and Reggie lay at her feet and saw the soft colour come and go on her cheek, saw the smile which lingered round her delicately-cut lips, envied the wind which ruffled her golden hair—noted all this with a strange, weary pain, trying to teach himself the lesson that this was the last of the brightness for him. In the long years to come he would have to rest content with these two stolen pleasures—a row on the river, an afternoon ramble in the woods.

He watched the small white hands as they deftly put the flowers together; but it was Grisel who broke the long silence at last.

"There," she said. "I hope you admire my handiwork. I have made one for myself and one for some one else."

She held up two dainty bouquets of delicate anemones for his inspection and admiration.

"Thank you, La Grise. I shall keep it."

"But you are not the 'some one' I meant. It was Jack. I thought it would please him."

"And do you not think it would please me also, La Grise? Do give it to me as a remembrance of our last walk together."

"Rather a fading remembrance, after all," she said. "I hope it will not be as transient in duration as the flowers."

"How long is it since your first ball, Grisette?"

She looked astonished at the irrelevance of the question. "Four years," she answered.

"And I have a spray of faded orange blossom, and the perfume still lingers round it, and brings back a bright picture to my mind. I would not part with it for worlds," he continued, and his voice had grown dangerously low and thrilling. His eyes rested on her face, and he saw the colour rising to her temples as she turned away her head.

"Keepsakes are an absolute mistake," she said, springing to her feet, and tossing the two bunches of anemones far out of reach among the grass.

"I burnt my spray of orange blossom only last night. I advise you to do the same."

Reggie had risen also to his feet, surprised by her sudden vehemence, and reminded also of how far he had gone by the faint scorn which curled Grisel's lip.

"You are right," he said. "Does that satisfy you?"

He had taken his orange blossom from an old letter-case he carried with him, and strewed it in fragments at his feet.

Grisel was standing with her face averted. She turned suddenly round at the sound of his hurt voice, and held out her hand.

"Oh, Le Gris, forgive me! I did not mean to be cross!"

"You are forgiven, my queen," he said, and raised the hand she had held out to him to his lips.

After that, they discovered that they were already late of starting for the station, and before Philip and Bryde had been found more time was lost.

They only arrived on the platform as the train steamed in and set down its one first-class passenger in the shape of Jack and his luggage. He was looking in better spirits than usual, and joined heartily in the general chatter, when, having confided Mr. Hunt's luggage to the care of the station-master, they turned their backs on the station for their two miles' walk—a long, flat, dusty road, with hedges at either side. So it was for a mile and a-half; then as it neared the Manor it took a sudden turn, and all at once one found oneself away from the glare of the dusty road, and in the cool shade of the Bramleigh woods. Rather under the road was heard the continuous roar of the river as it fell over the lasher near the home farm.

They had nearly got over the first mile and a-half of their dusty walk without almost noticing the disagreeables of the way, so eager and animated were they in the interchange of home news; and Jack was anxious to hear of Reggie's home-coming and arrival.

Suddenly they became conscious of the sound

of wheels approaching at an unusually rapid pace. At first nothing was to be seen but a cloud of dust some half-mile away; then, as it approached, they distinguished a single figure sitting in the vehicle, whatever it was.

"It is a runaway!" exclaimed Philip; and certainly there was no doubt of the fact. The tremendous pace at which it was coming, and the wild way the carriage was thrown from side to side of the road, left but little hope of either carriage or occupant being saved.

There were a few minutes of horrible suspense. The road in some parts was so narrow that, as it advanced nearer, it seemed hardly possible that the walking party could escape unhurt.

It was near enough now to distinguish more clearly. "Good God, it is Sybil!" exclaimed Reggie.

"It must be stopped before the turn of the road, or——"

Jack's voice did not finish the sentence. All knew only too well that if no help came before the turn, the carriage and all must go over the

bank into the river. They saw that Sybil
had hold of the reins, and to a certain extent
was able to guide the horses. Philip had
placed Bryde behind him under shelter of the
hedge, but Grisel unconsciously clung to Reggie's
hand as he stood beside her. Jack had crossed
the road, and stood a few yards further down,
nearer the dreaded corner. On came the phaeton
at terrific speed. They could hear the hard
breathing of the chestnuts, they could see the
still, white terror on Sybil's face, as she exerted
all her strength to guide the horses in safety
past her sisters. She evinced no personal fear,
though she must have known as well as they
did what lay before her.

A few seconds more of breathless suspense,
and then Grisel felt herself suddenly drawn
back by a strong arm, and held in safety by
her sister.

A whirlwind of dust, a clatter of horses' feet,
a half-stoppage, and the carriage passed on;
another second, and then a pause.

Grisel had covered her face with her hands

to shut out what she feared was coming. She looked up now, and with a wild cry of " Le Gris !" fell fainting on the road.

He had sprung forward first, had almost succeeded, when he was hit by the shaft. The carriage passed on, leaving him senseless where he had been knocked down. A few yards further on, a few moments before certain destruction, Jack had succeeded in stopping the horses; their first check had broken the pace at which they were going. They stood now, flecked with foam, but quiet, evidently relieved that their temporary madness was over.

Sybil leaped from the phaeton, and hurried back to where Grisel was lying. Reggie had already risen. He had been but partially stunned, and, save for a severe bruise on the shoulder, did not seem much hurt. So the accident, which might have had such serious consequences, was but a trivial one after all, if Grisel would but awaken from her long death-like faint.

Jack, in anxiety, raised Grisel from where she had fallen. Philip was holding the horses, while

Reggie hurried to a neighbouring cottage for water.

She lay on the bank, with her head resting on Sybil's knee, white and still. At last came a sigh, a trembling of her eyelids, and she opened her eyes. She looked round questioningly, as she tried to rise from her recumbent position; then suddenly the pallor returned to her cheek, as her memory came back to her.

"Oh! where is Le Gris? What has happened?" she asked, feebly.

"He is quite safe, Grisette, and has gone in search of water for you." It was Jack who spoke, but she still looked puzzled. "He was knocked over, but not hurt. If you had not been such a foolish child you would have seen it for yourself," he added, gently.

"I am sorry I was so foolish," she said; and Reggie returning at the moment, she took the water he had brought with tremulous thanks, and then declared she was better, and able to go home.

"You should feel flattered, Mainwaring, at a

young lady going off into a genuine faint, no humbug about it, because she had the misfortune to be eyewitness of your overthrow," said Philip, thoughtlessly, intent only on bringing a smile to Grisel's white face.

There was a moment's pause before Reggie answered.

"I am sorry I should have been the cause of it," was all he said, carefully avoiding Grisel's eye as he answered.

The crimson had risen in a flood and dyed Grisel's throat and cheek. In her confusion she tried to rise to her feet; she was still unable to do so, and nearly fainted again in the attempt.

Jack looked from one to the other. A spasm of pain shot across his face, but no trace of unusual feeling was discernible in his voice as he said—

"Grisette, will you let me drive you home?"

"Oh yes, please do!" she answered, gratefully.

CHAPTER IX.

NOT AS A WOMAN.

THE day after, Reggie came early to the Manor to inquire if Grisel were better. She had not left her room when he arrived, and it was Sybil who answered his inquiries. He was much distressed to hear that she was still far from well. Sybil had always known of his love for her sister; before her he never attempted to disguise his real feelings.

Sybil had resolved to give him a word of warning, if she had but an opportunity; she summoned her courage to speak as he was leaving that morning.

"Reggie, I have been thinking that it would be better for *you* if you did not come here so often during the next three weeks."

"Never mind me. I know I am laying up more pain for myself in the future; but I have counted the cost, Sybil, and the pleasure outweighs the pain."

"But it is not only for you," she said, hesitatingly; "it is for everyone concerned; better, in fact, for Grisel," she added, in desperation.

Reggie was silent a moment, then:

"Thank you for telling me this; I shall come as seldom as possible," he said.

"You are sure you are not angry with me, Le Gris? Long ago you know what we all hoped for; but, as things now are, it is better that you should keep away; and you are sure you do not think me unkind?"

"Unkind! No. You and I have always been friends. It was good of you to speak. I thought I was only bringing danger on myself, and I took the risk of that."

"I do not think it is exactly danger for her. Perhaps it is only my stupidity which makes mountains of mole-hills; only it cannot do any harm to stay away just for three weeks."

So Reggie was dismissed from the Manor for three weeks only. He supposed he would be there with danger to no one on Grisel's wedding day.

Fortunately, or unfortunately, his father was not so well again, and he had not much time for self-grievance.

Grisel was much surprised and perplexed at Reggie's continued absence. She did not say much about it. She knew his father was ill, and yet she grudged losing him for the last few weeks. She had never dared to question herself closely regarding the revelation which had almost come to her when she saw Reggie thrown down, and, as she thought, killed. She was hardly conscious of how jealously she watched against any reference to it in her own mind; and, for the few days immediately following the accident, she was able for so little exertion, and went about so listless and weary, so unlike her usual self, that Jack, whose holiday was drawing to a close, gave up all other engagements to be constantly with her, giving her but little time to read her feelings aright.

It was well perhaps; who can answer such things? Never, in all the four years that Jack had been engaged to her, had she been half as lovable in his eyes as now, when suddenly she had become so much more dependent upon him. She was entwining herself more and more round his heart, and since his talk with Lenore a desperate longing had seized on him for their speedy marriage. Grisel, she had said, would teach him the higher life; her child-like faith would lead him onwards in paths which he had not yet trod.

He ventured to say something of this to Grisel herself. It was the evening before he returned to town, and she had slipped away from the general chatter and noise going on in the drawing-room, where Philip, having found an old cornet, was trying to coax music out of it, and was soothing her aching head and restlessness as her hands wandered listlessly over the keys of the schoolroom piano.

Has Romney Manor ever yet been described?
A large two-storied house, with quaint Eliza-
bethan oak front, and all the principal rooms
on the ground floor, oak lined and floored, in
keeping with the façade.

A very long, straight avenue was the usual
approach; but winding among the woods and
rolling park came another and smaller entrance,
the shortest cut to Bramleigh, and used only, as
a rule, by the Mainwarings; this latter passed
close beside the schoolroom window, which, like
the rest of the rooms, opened directly on the
lawn.

And it was to the schoolroom that Grisel had
fled, with the strange, unaccountable sadness
hanging over her. It was late, very nearly
eleven o'clock; daylight had gone, and was
replaced by a soft, green light, which made the
spruce firs stand out black and feathery against
the sky—like hearse plumes, thought Grisel;
and then she smiled at her own morbid thoughts,
and played on softly to herself, forgetting her
weariness and vexation as the exquisite chords

and harmonies of the old Latin hymns thrilled through her.

Then in the stillness she began to sing. The room was far from the others; no one would be disturbed. Her voice rose and fell full of richness and purity, filling the otherwise empty room. She was singing as no one had ever heard her sing, with a passionate feeling that surprised herself. What were the words? Only one of her favourite hymns, which she had begun unconsciously:

"E'en though it be a cross that raiseth me,
Still all my song shall be, nearer, my God, to Thee!
Nearer to Thee!"

Jack had left the drawing-room soon after her disappearance; he had guessed where she had flown, and followed her. Now he stood spellbound, listening to her voice—Grisel's voice as he had never heard it before, when over and over again she had sung to him from her quaint collection of brightly-coloured scraps; but her rendering of sacred music was something new to him. He and she had rarely spoken on graver subjects; she, because she thought him so much better and older and above her in everything that she was shy of introducing the topic, and Jack had not thought of doing so himself. He had looked on her as a child whose life was so pure and bright that religion came to her as unconsciously as the air she breathed; he was startled at finding in her the soul-thrilling power which prayed for pain even, if so she could reach to higher things.

Of the two women he had known and loved during his life, both he discovered were actuated by the same ruling principle. Yes, Lenore was right! Grisel was mortal enough to understand and sympathise with his hitherto loveless life.

Grisel sang on unconscious of her audience, and he stood listening and waiting until she should cease; but he must have made some sound at last, for Grisel stopped suddenly and turned round.

"I thought I was alone," she said. "Have you been here long?"

"No, not long. You are not going to stop

because I have come? I will go again, Grisette, if you wish it."

She had risen from the piano and crossed the room to the open door.

"I am not going to sing again, Jack, but do not go away. Come out on the terrace; it is such a perfect evening, and it is cooler than in-doors."

He followed her out into the starlight, and stood beside her as she found a seat in an old oak niche under the window. She sat with her hands clasped across her knee—a small white figure, and her profile stood out clearly against the background of the evening sky.

"Are you better to-night, Grisette?" he asked at last.

"I suppose so; there is really nothing the matter with me!"

"You may say that, child, but you are not like yourself just now. I never before heard you sing as you were doing when I caught you without your knowledge. What have you got to do with such earth-weary feelings—you whose life ought to be continual sunshine?"

" The sunshine has gone out of my life lately ;
but do not mind, Jack dear, it will all come back
again soon.   Perhaps I have too little to do ; in
a few weeks my hands will be very full of
business !"

She looked up at him as she spoke, and smiled ;
but he was gazing away past her, and did not
seem to have heard the latter half of her speech.
He turned suddenly at last, and in the dim light
she could see how eager and anxious he was for
the reply to his question.

" Grisel, why did you sing those words as I
entered ?"

" What words ?" she asked.

" ' E'en though it be a cross that raiseth me.'
What do you know of crosses or pain ?"

" Did I sing them ?   Ah yes, I remember.
They are favourite words of mine," she said,
dreamily.

" I might make them mine, Grisette dearest ;
but you, such thoughts are not for your pure
life !"

" Jack, you who are so good, so far above me

in everything, I always feel so small beside you, and try continually to improve a little to be fit for you."

"To be fit for you!" Her words startled him. Why would she look up to him so, putting him on a pedestal, when he longed to learn from her? Was their life to be god and worshipper, and not "Come, fellow-being, love and work with me"? He knew he was no demi-god even. If she could look back over the history of the past ten years, how she would cover her eyes and shudder! Others might not have called it a much-stained page, but he, standing there beside her girlish innocence, felt the smallest sins rise in judgment against him.

She wondered at his long silence; she continued her last sentence as if there had been no pause.

"However, Jack, surely in a few years, being constantly with you, you will be able to make something of me."

She spoke more lightly, trying to dispel the cloud which rested on his brow.

"You must not speak so, Grisette; you do not know what you say." He spoke with passionate eagerness. "It is not I who must teach, but must learn. You know nothing of my real self; you would be shocked, stunned, if you could look into my past. You say you are trying to mould your life to be fit for me, when in reality you should draw closer round you the garments of your spotless womanhood that they might not be soiled as I went by!" He stopped, and she in her wonderment had risen to her feet.

"What do you mean?" she asked. "I can never believe anything bad of you. You are dreaming, Jack; you are trying to startle me. But, if in truth you are as bad as you say, we are all wicked, you know." Then she added, reverently, "I need not tell you where we ought to take all our badness and blackness and lay it at His feet. There is God!"

"But if I do not believe in Him, Grisel? If religion is but an empty shell to me, the shell forming the covering to hang my morality and respectability upon, but inside no life, all void,

desolate, and the moan sounding in the emptiness
as the voice of the sea, a continual unrest?"

She had started back when he first began
to speak, and looked at him with wondering
eyes.

"Do I frighten you, my darling?" he said,
putting his arm round her and drawing her close
to his side. "I am no worse than many others,
Grisette. Don't you pity me? My mother died
when I was born, and there was no one to teach
me the religion you love. How can I believe,
unless *you* will teach me?"

"Oh, that will never do! Sybil must tell you
all about it, Jack. I am so stupid, I never could
make it all clear to you. She is so good; better
than anyone I know. I could not teach you.
I dare not do it!"

She had disengaged herself from his arms in
her earnest pleading, and he let her go—despair
chilling him through and through.

"If you cannot make me believe, Grisette, I
must give it up. I suppose I shall get through
what is left of this life fairly well, as until now

I have succeeded in doing; and for the next world, let that wait. Who knows if there is one?"

He saw the tears trembling on her eyelashes, and her white, sorrowful face looked wistful and pleading as she drew a step nearer to him and laid her hand on his arm.

"Have I hurt you, Jack? I did not mean to do so; but if you are content with what I can tell you I will do my best, and you must promise never, never to speak again as you did just now, as you know you do not believe what you said. Will this satisfy you?"

"Oh, Grisette, my darling, if you knew what a woman's love can do, you would not despair. Such love can save a soul!"

He had taken her in his arms, and held her as if he would never let her go.

"What is such love? have I ever felt it?" she exclaimed, feebly; but he stopped her words with kisses, and she stood passive and unresisting, overwhelmed by the strength of his feeling.

So they remained both silent, and in the silence

a sound broke on the air. Both heard it, and forgot themselves in listening.

"It is coming nearer," said Grisel; "who can it be at this hour? it is nearly twelve o'clock."

"Some one from Bramleigh," Jack said, with a presentiment of coming sorrow rising in him.

Distinctly could be heard the sharp, rapid trot of a horse, and the roll of wheels.

"It must be Reggie; no one drives at such a pace as he does. What can be the matter?"

They stood listening; they were within the doorway; and a moment after, something drove quickly past. Grisel's heart stood still, for she had recognised the dogcart as Reggie's.

A moment after, the loud peal of the hall-door bell echoed through the house, startling the inmates, and bringing them from different parts to see what had happened.

The drawing-room party were already collected when Grisel and Jack joined them, and this was what they saw: Mr. Romney had retired to his room, and now from the unexpected summons had re-emerged in dressing gown and slippers.

Around him were gathered the quintette who had been cornet-practising, and from various unnamed doors heads were appearing to satisfy their curiosity.

The door was being unbarred, having been closed for the night, and as the rattling chain fell from the lock, Reggie Mainwaring sprang into the hall, impatient at even the momentary delay.

"Where is La Grise?" he said, looking round. "My father is worse, and calls continually for her. Will you spare her to us, Mr. Romney? I will bring her safely back to-morrow, and nothing else will satisfy him."

"Of course, of course. Grisel, get ready directly; and, Reggie, come and have some wine and water while she wraps herself up. Tell me of your father. When did this change come?"

"Some few hours ago. I was most unwilling to disturb you all, but nothing else will satisfy him, and my mother thought you would understand our anxiety."

A few minutes elapsed before Grisel reappeared.

She was very quiet, and looked a strange little figure in the all-enveloping cloak in which Sybil had wrapped her.

"I am quite ready now, Le Gris. We had better go at once."

She kissed her father and sisters, and Jack carefully wrapped the rug round her as Reggie took the driver's seat. She bent down as they were starting, and held out her hand.

"Jack," she said, "you will not go to-morrow; you must wait till I come back."

"I will wait, Grisette. Do not hurry back for me; you are in good hands."

"I will look well after her, Hunt; and you will have her returned to you to-morrow."

That was all. A crack of the whip, and they were off as rapidly as the dogcart had come.

The home party dispersed to their rooms with a strange sense of unreality about it all.

CHAPTER X.

THE TRUTH AT LAST.

IT was a strange drive for both Reggie and Grisel — neither spoke for some time. She supposed he was silent from anxiety about his father; she did not like to disturb him with useless questions, so she relapsed into thought. The scene of the evening occupied her mind. She was overwhelmed with what her lover had told her; she felt weak, childish, helpless before such unbelief. And he had said, "Such love can save a soul." Her love! It was impossible!

She began to examine into the strength of her love, to test it with imaginary trials. She shivered as she found how little it would stand. "I would do almost anything for him because he loves me so, but I wish——"

The wish was never expressed in thought even; they had turned in at the Bramleigh Hall gates, and the gravel crunched under the wheels. At the sound of their return, hurrying lights were seen in the passages; the inmates were on the alert.

"You will find my father much changed, La Grise." They were the first words either had spoken. "His memory has failed completely, and we had hoped that his wish to see you would have passed away like similar fancies; but, as his mind became clearer, this evening he recurred again and again to his desire that you should be sent for."

"Dear Sir Roger! I have not seen him for so many months, and at one time I was continually with him. I am glad you came for me, Le Gris. I would do anything for your father and mother."

"Yes, La Grise, he always looked on you as a daughter. I suppose he wished to see you once more; he has not said anything to lead us to any other conclusion."

K

"Is he so ill as that?" Grisel's voice was awe-struck. "Oh! he must get well again!"

"I fear not, Grisette. My father is eighty years of age. He is five-and-twenty years older than my mother."

"Poor Lady Mainwaring! I am sorry for her."

"You must comfort her, La Grise. She is dreadfully distressed. The doctors told her this evening that there was no hope of my father's recovery; it is a question only of hours."

They had drawn up at the side door, that their arrival might not disturb the sufferer. Reggie lifted Grisel carefully down, and led her into the hall, where the housekeeper was waiting to see that she was properly cared for.

"How is Sir Roger now?" Reggie asked.

"Much the same, sir. Her ladyship is with him. She said Miss Romney was to have some tea after her drive."

"Oh! I do not wish any tea, thank you. I would rather go to Sir Roger."

"La Grise, you must go with Mrs. Newton and

have something to eat. You know I promised to take care of you."

Reggie spoke authoritatively, and Grisel obeyed at once. She was taken into Lady Mainwaring's private sitting-room, and Mrs. Newton stood by while she ate a biscuit and drank the tea, telling her all the time how thankful everyone was that she had come; that they had been saying perhaps, since she was engaged to another gentleman, she might not care so much about it at all; but somehow she had been sure all the time they were speaking that Miss Grisel was certain to come, especially when Mr. Reginald had gone for her himself. As she stopped speaking, Reggie himself appeared.

"Can you come now, La Grise? My father has been asleep, and is awake again. He sleeps so much, it is better that you should come to him at once."

She rose and followed him, without a word, up the dimly-lighted staircase, with a strange hush pervading the air. Reggie gently turned the handle of a door, and she found herself in Sir Roger's dressing-room. The door of the adjoining room stood open, and, at the sound of their entrance, Lady Mainwaring came out from the inner apartment. She was very pale and worn-looking from long watching; dark shadows were under her eyes, which were bright and shining with excitement.

"This is good of you, little Grisel," she said, taking the girl's face between her hands and kissing her on the forehead. "Dear Sir Roger has been asking for you continually; he will be satisfied now you are here. He is very weak, and will perhaps hardly know you at first," she added, as she led the way into the sick-room.

Grisel had never seen great sickness before; she had never been in a room with one even near to his last journey. She drew back, half in awe, as Lady Mainwaring pushed aside the curtains of the bed.

But there was nothing there to fear; all so peaceful, a gentle sleeping away.

The old man was propped up with pillows to

alleviate his oppressed breathing; his eyes were closed, and, save for the anxiety printed on the faces of those watching, there was nothing to tell that his course was nearly run.

Grisel turned involuntarily to Reggie, begging him with her eyes to keep beside her; all was strange and solemn to her, and this, coming after the exciting scene she had previously passed through, was almost too much for her composure.

There was silence in the room, save for the heavy breathing of the sufferer; waiting was written on the faces and in the attitudes of those beside the bed. Lady Mainwaring, with eyes bent only on her husband, and Reggie, watching Grisel, thinking that if things had been as he once dreamed, she would have been standing there, as now, Sir Roger's daughter, and his wife. Sir Roger opened his eyes. They wandered sightlessly round the room; a gleam of recognition lighted up his face as they rested a moment on his wife.

"Grisel, little Grisel; has she come yet?"

The tones were feeble, the accent full of questioning anxiety. " Has little Grisel come ?"

" I am here, dear Sir Roger. Do not you see me, close beside you ?"

At the sound of her voice he slowly turned his head, and she took one of the weary, time-lined hands in her own. She bent low over the bed till her face came near to him.

" Do you know me now, dear Sir Roger ? Here I am, standing beside Reggie."

A smile hovered round his lips.

" That is right, beside Reggie, where you ought to be, my child. God bless you both. Yes, I am going very soon — eighty years of a happy life—and now it is but right that the old—should—make—way—for—the—young."

His eyes closed ; he had dozed off again. Reggie glanced at Grisel. She stood silent ; she had not been conscious of how Sir Roger's words might be construed.

Half-an-hour passed away without any change, save the gradual sinking of strength. They thought he would probably not speak again ;

but, unexpectedly, came a rally. He took some nourishment, and seemed anxious to say something.

They had to bend low to hear his words.

" Reggie, Grisel, come close to me," he whispered.

Then, suddenly, there was an accession of strength, and his words were heard clearly by all.

" I wanted to bless you both. Grisel, you will make him a good wife ; remember, he is my only child."

Grisel turned deadly white, but did not move from where she stood. Reggie came closer to her, and whispered low and eagerly—

" Forgive us, La Grise. We knew nothing of this."

She held out her hand in recognition of what he had said, but dared not turn and meet his pleading eyes. He took the hand she held out to him, and so, hand in hand, they stood. Sir Roger raised his and laid it on theirs. Reggie felt Grisel suddenly try to withdraw hers from his grasp. She dreaded what was coming.

"Do not disturb his last moments," pleadingly whispered Reggie. "It can make no difference to us, La Grise, and it will satisfy him."

She made no further opposition, and Lady Mainwaring thanked her silently. Then slowly and solemnly in the chamber of death came the old man's blessing, pronounced upon them as man and wife; and, as the words fell on her ear, Grisel at last knew the truth—knew that she loved Reggie as she had never loved before, and that day fortnight was her wedding-day.

The words of blessing were scarcely ended, when a change came over Sir Roger's face. He turned to his wife, his hand still resting on the clasped hands of Le Gris and La Grise; but for her who had been his everything for nearly thirty years was reserved the last look, the last smile.

"He is going," said the nurse.

"Oh! take me away; I cannot bear it, Le Gris." It was Grisel who spoke; she could hold up no longer.

Reggie led her away to the room which had

been prepared for her; and there, white and trembling, she sank into a chair.

"Can you ever forgive us, La Grise, for all this pain we have brought upon you?"

She looked up at him through her tear-filled eyes, and tried to smile forgiveness. Her voice was steadied with difficulty as she answered—

"You must go back to your father, Le Gris. Never mind me."

"Will my sister say she forgives me? I cannot leave her without."

"I forgive," she said faintly, and raised her eyes to his, so full of love, so brimming over with their own sad secret, that he might have read aright; but he was so sure that he had never been more to her than companion and friend, that he only read in them sorrow and sympathy for them all. He could not bear to leave her when he longed to take her in his arms and comfort her, and tell her that his father's words were but his own soul's desire; and yet his place was at his mother's side, by his father's deathbed.

He must go. He yielded to temptation and kissed her on the brow—no lover's kiss ; it rested there but a moment, and with it Reggie had gone.

Grisel never moved from where he had left her, alone in the dawn-lighted room to face the truth at last. His kiss had brought the crimson to her neck and brow. The knowledge of what he had become to her overwhelmed her with its power; it broke from her at last in a low wail of bitterness.

"What have I done, what have I done ? Why did I ever come here to-night ? Why did you let me come, Jack ? I would never have known, never have found out this dreadful thing that I have done. How could I love him when he does not care for me ? Oh ! Jack, why did you not make me love you more ? Now I know what you meant. 'Such love could save a soul.' This burning, bitter pain that might have been so sweet, must be stamped out at once. No one must ever find out how wrong I have been, and I meant no harm. I think I must have loved him always, and it was so much part of me that I never found it out. Oh! Jack, my poor Jack, you shall never drag this from me. I will be such a good wife to you, and in time you will teach me to forget."

She ceased her complaint, and sat silent and weary. The summer morn was forcing its way through the curtains, the air was broken by the song of birds. She did not know how time had passed. There was a sound in the house; all must be over. No one would come to her now. She took off her things and slipped sadly to bed.

CHAPTER XI.

A TRYING DAY.

A DULL, grey morning had succeeded the perfect evening, leaden clouds covered the sky, and a soft rain was steadily falling.

Sybil had risen early, the events of the previous day had made her sleepless, and now she was ready long before the rest of the household were awake.

She threw up her window, and the smell of the damp, thirsty earth filled her room. Things were bending under their weight of moisture. When does this world seem so thoroughly to rejoice as when the windows of heaven open after a long run of dry weather?

Sybil looked across the woods at the chimneys of Bramleigh just shown above the trees. The

smoke curled blue and lazily into the still air,
unable to dispel itself. It set her musing and
moralising. The time slipped past, sounds were
beginning to stir in the house, and a gentle
knock came to the door. She thought it was
the servant coming to awaken her, and did not
turn her head.

"Sybil, it's me," and the weary, dripping figure
of Grisel had entered the room.

Sybil started to her feet.

"Grisette, child, what has brought you?"

"Don't be angry with me, Syb dear. I was
so lonely, so unhappy, I could not help it."

And then the pent-up floods broke out, and
Grisel cried as if her heart were breaking.

Sybil did not speak. She took off Grisel's
hat and cloak, she soothed her like a child, and
then, leaving her for a few minutes, she returned
with something for her to eat and drink. She
watched while Grisel forced herself to swallow
a few mouthfuls. Gradually her sobs were at
longer intervals, and at last she looked up
through her tears and smiled. When she had

finished, Sybil took the plate and cup from her hand, and, drawing her chair beside her at the window, waited. Grisel spoke at last.

"He is dead, Sybil. I almost saw him die!"

"How glad you must be you went, Grisette."

"Am I? I hardly think so. I did no good."

Then came a pause. It was Grisel who again broke the silence.

"I have not seen Lady Mainwaring since; I came away before anyone was up; nobody knew I was going."

"Except Le Gris."

"Le Gris did not know either; no one knew, Sybil. I walked here, it is only two miles; and I could not stay, it was so dreadful."

"But, darling, it was over. It would have been better if you had waited till Le Gris drove you here."

"I couldn't, Sybil. They will not mind!"

"I am afraid they will think it strange you left without their knowledge." Sybil spoke very gently.

"Oh no, they will understand; I think they

would expect it. If you had been me, you would have done the same, Sybil; but I cannot tell you why."

"Very well, darling; I am sure it is all right."

Then they talked on in low voices about the old man who was dead. Grisel had always been to him as a daughter, his death was a personal sorrow to her, and Sybil encouraged her to speak, but she did not revert to the cause of her sudden flight from Bramleigh. Sybil was puzzled, but wisely refrained from alluding again to the subject; she knew that in all probability she would receive a solution in some way soon. She persuaded Grisel to lie down, and Grisel was only too glad to defer the evil day, if only by a few hours; she dreaded meeting them all, and much repented now having asked Jack to wait till she returned. How could she face him with her guilty secret? In a fortnight she would have grown more used to it.

Much surprise was evinced at the breakfast table when Sybil broke the news that Grisel had returned and Sir Roger was dead.

"How did she come? Did she walk, or did Reggie drive her?" asked a chorus of voices.

"She walked," Sybil answered from her place behind the tea-urn. "The child was lonely, and could bear it no longer; I have persuaded her to rest for a few hours. Jack, you will not leave till to-morrow, I hope?"

"It depends on the post-bag," he said; "but I hope not."

"After all, not a very long separation," remarked Philip. "Cheer up, old boy. Remember yesterday fortnight."

"I fear Sir Roger's death will be a great grief to Grisette," Jack answered, gravely.

"Lovers are a queer set," Philip went on. "I suggested a pleasant anticipation, and he can think of nothing but gloomy fears for Grisette."

"I suppose it is a natural thought under the circumstances," said Augusta.

"Ah yes, I forgot the circumstances. He is not to be judged by ordinary rules of humanity."

"As far as I am aware, Jack is not the only

one at table to be treated leniently because of circumstances," Mr. Romney remarked, drily, rising from the table and taking with him his spectacles and bundle of newspapers. While the laugh turned against Philip, Mr. Romney paused on his way to the study.

"I suppose the funeral will be within the week," he said. "Will you see that I have a *crêpe* hat-band, Sybil," and then he disappeared for his daily interview with his head man on the home farm.

A calm came over those left behind. The mention of the funeral had recalled the sad events of the night, and they felt that their mirth had been ill-timed.

They talked of probabilities resulting from Sir Roger's death, and discussed the subject of the will, as to what he had to leave, and where and to whom he would have left it.

They were in the middle of the discussion when a servant entered with a note for Sybil.

"Sir Reginald's groom is waiting for an answer," he said.

L

"How strange it sounds! I shall never remember to call Le Gris Sir Reginald," Bryde
remarked, and Sybil left the room to answer
the note. The rest of the party dispersed to
their various duties, Augusta linking her arm into
Bryde's and carrying her off for a long gossip.

"Aren't you coming to help me to smoke,
Bridget ?"

Bryde looked round wistfully.

"Not yet, Philip," answered Augusta ; "I require
her advice about various things."

"Never mind, Bryde ; go and discuss. I shall
be smoking in the garden for several hours."

" I wish you did not give way so much to that
abominable habit. You men are fit for nothing
unless you are smoking."

"Gently, gently, Gus ; don't teach Bryde to
exaggerate. Besides, I dare say you have some
pet luxury which you would not give up."

Bryde marched Augusta away from farther
discussion.

Reggie's note had been one of inquiry about
Grisel ; he was unable to be the bearer of it,

owing to having to make all arrangements. His mother and he had been much distressed at Grisel's return to the Manor. At the end of it, he said he would in all probability be at the Manor in the afternoon; would Sybil grant him a private interview?

The rain continued steadily all day, and none of the ladies left the house. Grisel had fallen asleep, and orders were given that she was not to be disturbed. The men had to content themselves with cigars in the hothouses, and a rat-hunt at the courtyard. Towards afternoon, they took to knocking about the balls in the billiard room. The Jerninghams, Bryde, and Jack were all collected there. Sybil was in the drawing-room expecting Reggie. She had several letters to write, and was not sorry for the excuse of being alone. It was nearly five o'clock before she was interrupted; she was so intent on her writing, that she did not hear Reggie's step on the gravel, and he had entered the room by the glass door before she was aware of his presence.

She rose from the table, going forward to meet him with words of sympathy on her lips for the loss he had sustained, but he hardly listened to what she said at first.

"You did not blame us, Sybil?" he exclaimed, as soon as she had ceased speaking. "It was not our fault; she left the house without our knowledge."

"She told me so; she took all blame on herself. I think she was overwrought, poor child. She fell asleep soon after she came home, and has not yet awakened. Of course, we did not blame you; but will not you sit down? I wish to hear all about Lady Mainwaring and your dear father's death. Do not fear interruption; the others are all in the billiard room, and will not disturb us."

He seated himself as desired; he seemed pre-occupied, and only spoke when Sybil addressed him.

"Was it sudden at the end? I hope he did not suffer?"

"No; no suffering. Yes, comparatively speaking, it was sudden. There had been no decided change for the worse until the afternoon."

"How terrible for poor Lady Mainwaring!"

"Yes, indeed. After eight-and-twenty years of a happy married life, the separation must be a terrible wrench."

"What a comfort it is that you are at home, Le Gris!"

"I am very thankful," he said. "She has quite broken down to-day. Her health has been much tried with the long watching and anxiety; as soon as she can be moved, I will take her away for change."

"I suppose it is too soon to have formed any plans?" Sybil said, interrogatively.

"Nothing definite yet. I spoke to her this morning of shutting up Bramleigh and going abroad for a year. I shall have, at any rate, to leave the army."

"You will dislike that very much, I fear."

"I shall miss regular occupation at first, but I could not go out to India again and leave my mother when there is no necessity for it in a money point of view; besides, Bramleigh is an estate which requires a great deal of time bestowed upon it. My father, up to the last few years of his life, saw into everything himself; latterly we had to get a steward, but he is not altogether satisfactory, and so I propose setting to work myself. One will feel one is at least trying to do some little good in the world by looking after one's tenantry."

"Then, also, think of your mother."

"Yes; I do not forget my poor mother; but Sybil," he added, half-eagerly, half-sorrowfully, "is it a heartless thing to say it is hard for a man to make his mother his chief interest?"

"I understand you, Reggie; but never mind the hardness. Remember it is always something given you to do."

"I suppose so," he answered, "yet one longs at times that things might be otherwise. However, in the meanwhile, we shall not return to Bramleigh for a year. I think the foreign plan is decidedly the best in every way. I do not think I could meet La Grise again after last night."

"I think it is as well, perhaps, that you should not meet till after her marriage."

"Yes," he answered, thoughtfully; then, after a pause, "I suppose she told you all?"

"I hardly think she did, Le Gris; she did not seem inclined to speak, and I did not ask her."

"Do you remember, Sybil, about ten days ago, begging me to keep away from you all, not only on my own account, but because there might also be danger for her?"

"Yes, I remember; I have no reason since for supposing I was right in what I did; but, Reggie, it could do no possible harm."

"It was in kindness you did it, Sybil, and you have probably saved me some pain; but now I know that I might have been here every day without danger to her. If you had seen her as I saw her last night, you would think as I do. She will not mind me telling you; but just before my dear father died, he became

conscious for some little while, and almost the
first words he uttered were, "Grisel, you will
make him a good wife."

"Poor Grisette! What did she do?"

"Nothing; she showed no apparent feeling.
Only for a moment, as my father laid his hand
on ours, she offered some slight resistance; and
then he gave us his blessing as he would have
done had she been my wife. Do not judge
hardly," he said, imploringly; "I could not bear
to disturb his last moments, and it could make
no difference to her. I felt to the bottom of
my soul what it might have been, but she has
forgiven me."

"Have you seen her alone since?" Sybil
asked.

"Yes; I took her from the room before my
father died, but she did not seem to understand
all that had passed; her whole thoughts were
centred on my mother and myself, her one
desire that I should go back to my father and
not mind her; so I left her, and in the morning
we found she had gone."

They both sat silent for some little time. Sybil was beginning to read her sister's flight aright, and her whole being was filled with dismay at the turn things were taking.

There were sounds in the passage, the rain had cleared off, and the billiard party were going for a walk. Some time after, the Jerninghams and Bryde passed the window; Jack was not with them.

The voices of the trio broke upon the silence which had fallen on Reggie and Sybil; he rose to his feet and held out his hand.

" Well," he said, " I suppose I must say good-bye. We shall start immediately after the funeral, so I shall not be here again. Give all kind messages from me to your sisters; I shall see Mr. Romney again at the funeral."

" Good-bye, Reggie, I cannot tell how I feel for you, but you must try and forget all about us; we have not brought you much brightness."

" Do not say that; by far the happiest days of my life I have spent here; they will ever bring back to me thoughts of all the kindness I have met with from you all."

"Perhaps," he continued, "it is but a foolish surmise, but I have often wondered if I had never gone to India whether I could have made her love me. In the old days I was not wholly indifferent to her, at least I thought so; but she heard my father's words unmoved last night. If I had ever been more to her than now, surely she must have given some sign; and, Sybil, I am mad enough, fool enough, to love Grisette still. Thank God, she will never know it!"

And with that he was gone.

CHAPTER XII.

FOR THE SECOND TIME.

SOME half-hour previously Jack had left the billiard room. He thought he heard steps in Grisel's room, which was immediately above them. She would in all likelihood go at once to the drawing - room. Some unexplained instinct suggested to him that she ought to be warned that Sybil was not alone.

He waited for some minutes in the hall. There was no further sound; he must have been mistaken. But no; there was the cautious opening and shutting of a door, and then a quick, noiseless step was heard. It approached, and Grisel appeared with her hat on. She started as she saw Jack.

"I thought you were all gone out," she said.

"I waited for you, Grisette. Do you wish to go alone, or may I come with you?"

"I am only going as far as the garden. If you would like a walk, do not wait for me, Jack."

"I would rather come with you. Besides, you are far too white-faced a little mortal to go out alone. I must come and take care of you."

They passed silently out of the house and along the yew-hedged walks side by side. But neither spoke. Grisel walked wearily. Jack noticed it, and drew her hand within his arm. An almost imperceptible tremor passed through her. He felt it, and turned anxiously to her.

"You are utterly knocked up, my darling. I wish I had never let you go last night."

"Oh, Jack, if you had only said no! I should have been so thankful!"

He looked surprised at her vehemence.

"If I had had any idea that you were acting contrary to your wishes, I should have interfered.

But, darling, I thought you would wish to go.
Reggie ought to have been more considerate."

"It was not his fault. Oh no! It was no
one's fault. But, Jack, do not speak of it again.
I cannot even bear to think of it."

Gradually, he tried to draw her thoughts away
from the events of the past night, wishing to
interest her in their wedding tour. Grisel had
never been abroad. They had spent many happy
hours in planning their tour, what to see and
what to miss; but now all the plans failed to
interest her. It evidently required an effort
to concentrate her thoughts at all on what Jack
was saying.

He was perplexed and distressed, he did not
know how to deal with her. All his attempts
were fruitless; he desisted at last, and left her
in silence.

So they paced up and down the garden walks.
Everything was dripping from the rain, and heavy,
silver-lined clouds were hanging about. Grisel
felt the day in keeping with her own sad
thoughts. She wondered at the sun making

such efforts to come out. Why did it not leave her surrounded with darkness and gloom? The rain was only now clearing off the low-lying country, and across the heavy masses of vapour a rainbow appeared — a brilliant bow of colour on the sky. Grisel noted it, and tears filled her eyes. She read in it only cruel irony, which bid her hope ; and Jack noted it also, and from out the stories of his childhood rose the Bible narrative of the sign.

They come to all, those back-goings into the first years, when everything was so easily believed in perfect simplicity. They come with a softening influence, suggesting what the man was and what he has become.

Even the most hardened have these times of retrospect ; much more Jack, who was so utterly dissatisfied with his present existence. Poor fellow! His life had been one long tossing on a very restless sea ; and for the moment, as he saw the message of hope spanning the sky, as he felt the home influence of his surroundings, as he dreamt of the love and sympathy which were so soon to be his, who shall wonder at his mind being filled with the sense that his happiness had come at last? He turned to Grisel with the longing that she could read his thoughts aright.

"It is going to rain again," she said; "sunshine only comes in gleams."

She spoke truth. The clouds were closing in, and the momentary brightness was passing away. Heavy drops of rain began to fall, and they turned their steps in the direction of the house.

Both were occupied with their own thoughts. Neither noticed that the drawing-room window was open, nor did they heed the murmur of voices which came to them from the room.

Jack had not told Grisel that Reggie was with Sybil. All memory of it had passed from his mind, or he would not so willingly have guided her by the path he did. And those within were unconscious how, in the earnest and heat of their talk, their voices had risen above the level of their usual tones.

Slowly along the path came Jack and Grisel;

they were nearly at the open window now.
Grisel started as Reggie's voice caught her ear;
involuntarily they advanced another yard, and
then came the fatal words, which at once and
for ever dispelled Jack's dream.

Both heard Le Gris's wild tones; both stood
rooted to the spot, as they rang distinct and
clear across the air.

"And, Sybil, I am fool enough, mad enough,
to love Grisette still. Thank God, she will
never know it!"

A moment's awful silence, in which their hearts
stood still; then came the slam of the door as
Reggie left the room. It woke them from their
trance; it told Grisel that he whom she loved
loved her, and was gone. She forgot Jack, who
stood at her side; forgot all but the glad words
she had heard, bringing to her such a wonderful
vista of happiness.

"Le Gris, I am here!" she cried.

But no voice answered. Reggie was beyond
reach of her call; he had left the house, and
for a year.

And in the silence which followed, Grisel knew
what she had done; knew that she had betrayed
her secret. Before Jack could stop her, she had
fled; fled and hidden herself away in the Four
Aunts Gallery, and there, seated under the shadow
of her unhappy ancestress, she tried to understand what had happened.

Was it joy or sorrow which broke from her
in those heartrending sobs? She could not tell.
But this she knew, her whole being was glowing
with thankfulness that Reggie loved her. She
felt that she could act out her part now, content
with the knowledge she had gained. It seemed
such happiness, after the last twenty-four hours'
misery; it did not at the first strike her how
much sweeter it might have been.

Then, disentangling itself from out her thoughts,
came the remembrance of the scene she had
just passed through. Would it be so easy to
hide all from her future husband, or had she
already let him know? She trembled; he would
be so angry with her; in fact, they all would
be angry at what she had done. She looked

M

round in fear as she heard a step ascending
the staircase; she could not be mistaken in
the quick, firm tread. She buried her face in
her hands, and waited for what must follow.

He came up to where she sat, and stood there
in silence. He heard her stifled sobs, and no
softening came into the hard, grave lines around
his mouth; he folded his arms, and gazed down
on her. She was not his to touch and comfort.
The wish even to make her his own had passed
from him as he heard the half confession fall
from her lips, and now nought remained but to
part.

"Grisette, I have come to say good-bye, and to
set you free."

"Are you very angry with me," she whispered.

"Not angry, child; only sad."

"And it is my fault! Oh, Jack, do try and
forget this—forget what Reggie said. I am so
fond of you, Jack dear; if you will only forget,
I will still make you a good wife. Try me;
do!"

"You do not know what you are saying, Grisel.

You do not understand the weight of the burden that you are proposing to take upon your shoulders."

"I think I do," she murmured so low that he hardly heard the quiet determination of her tones.

"Remember," he continued, "it would be no sharp short struggle, no pain to be passed through and then lived down, but a daily, nay hourly, knowledge that you had made a mistake in your life, not only known to yourself, but aware also that I knew it too; and, hardest of all to bear perhaps, there would ever be recurring a contrasting of your happiness attained and unattainable."

Grisel sat perfectly still while he spoke. She did not raise her head to meet his eyes; she dreaded to see the pain written in them. When at last he was silent, she said—

"In time, I should forget. Time works wonders, you know; and it would be even harder to live with the knowledge that I had spoilt your life."

"That you would not do, child. I have my

work to live for; I will make it my mistress;
it shall absorb my powers of mind and body.
The monotony of the daily round and advancing
years will bring at least contentment, and the
consciousness that my sad-coloured existence
has not marred your life will be recompense
sufficient."

He ceased speaking, in wonder at his own
calmness. What had come to him? Was
it only in word, or that he really did not
care?

There was none of the maddening pain with
which he had parted from Lenore, none of the
wild longing to defy fate at any price. He had
held Grisel's love in his hand for years, and as
he was about to taste the cup he had waited for
so long, he had to set it down again untasted,
hardly lingeringly even. He stood before the girl
who was in a fortnight's time to have been his
wife, and went over again in memory their strange
introduction and acquaintance.

"Do you remember the spaewife's fable, La
Grise? It will come true after all. Why did

we not take her warning? We should have been saved some pain."

"Yes," she answered, and raised her head from her hands, looking up sadly at the face on the canvas above her, in its quaint, white satin robe, the snowy arms and neck gleaming in the darkly-lighted corridor. "You told me you did not believe her; you laughed at my ever repeating such nonsense; you said the third generation broke the spell, and I was so glad to believe you."

"But fate has proved too hard for us, Grisette. I defied it, and it has come back upon me. Enough of this. One thing, Grisel, you will find, not lose, your happiness, as Griselda de Grey did hers."

"Oh! Jack," she cried, piteously, "do not make out that I am utterly heartless. You seem to think that I do not care for the pain you are suffering; I am thinking only of you, not of myself, for now I know what pain love is."

She stood beside him, looking so worn and thin, so unlike her girlish brightness; she laid her hand on his arm, and looked wistfully away into vacancy.

"If you would only trust me!" she said. "I am sure I could make you happy."

"The thing is absurd, child," he answered, almost impatiently. "Do you think for a moment that either of us could so find our happiness? No, such can never be. In the future, we may some day meet as friends. Good-bye, child; forget me, and be happy."

He took both her small, quivering hands in his, and gave her one last kiss of farewell, and turned away. She hardly realised what had happened; she roused herself as his footsteps echoed in the passage.

"Oh! Jack, is this all?" she cried. "Are you really leaving me? Are you not going to trust me?"

He turned at the sound of her voice, and came once more to her side.

"It is best for all, little Grisel—best that I should leave you at once. Will you say good-bye, and let us part as friends?"

"Only friends, Jack? It seems so common-place, so little, after all we have been to each other."

"Grisette, do you not yet know your own heart, child? Some one is already much more to you than I can ever be. Think for a moment of Le Gris!"

As he saw the colour deepen on her cheek, and her eyes drop in consciousness of the secret they would tell, he felt how utterly incapable he had ever been to rouse in her the love he craved for. He saw it now, as she stood before him in all her beauty, with the knowledge of her love showing itself in every line of her speaking face. Yes, another had gained what he desired.

"Oh, Grisette," he exclaimed, "if I could only have made you love me so." He seized both her hands in a long, close pressure, and in a moment he was gone.

Sybil was alone in the drawing-room. She was so engrossed with Reggie's sorrow that she had hardly heard Grisel's cry; and now, when suddenly the door was opened and Jack entered, looking utterly unlike his usual self, she did not connect the two in thought.

"What has happened?" she asked, anxiously.

"Nothing," he said, "at least nothing that can signify to anyone but me. Sybil, all is at an end between us. Grisel and I have come to an understanding, and I have set her free."

"Free? What do you mean?"

"Had you no idea, Sybil, that I was not first in your sister's thoughts?"

Sybil did not answer; her suspicions aroused only that morning kept her silent.

"Then you did know! Oh, Sybil, was it fair to me not to have spoken? Think how close our marriage had come."

"Do you really mean that all is at an end?"

"All. I leave within an hour. You will probably never see me again."

He gave her some account of what had passed, but did not seem to wish to enter on details. He must see Mr. Romney, he said, and explain it to him.

"You can put all blame on me, Sybil; say what you like. I have jilted her perhaps would sound best, and give the neighbours somewhat to talk about. They are all to be pitied that they will miss the excitement of the wedding-day; it is but fair that they should have some gossip as amends."

"Oh! Jack, is that fair? You know how we must feel this. You have acted generously, nobly. We must bear the blame."

"My shoulders are broad enough. It matters little to me, either here or there. I care not for the world's kind judgment. Besides, it will be but a nine days' talk. Grisel will marry soon, and then who will trouble their heads about a simple Jack Hunt?"

CHAPTER XIII.

TWO ELDERLY LADIES.

JACK left the room. It wanted but an hour from the starting of the evening train for London. He must collect his things if possible before then. He did not wish to be present at the family dinner; he would rather see none of them again.

But fate decreed otherwise. In the passage he met Bryde and the Jerninghams just returned from walking.

"Goodness! Jack, you look as if you had seen a ghost. What's the matter with you?"

"I am rather in a hurry, Phil; I am going up by the night train to town."

"To town?" exclaimed all three.

"Yes," he said; "an alteration in my plans obliges me to leave to-night. I suppose I had better wish you all good-bye."

His manner was nervous and hurried; they shook the proffered hand in silence, and he passed to his room.

All three looked at one another.

"Something's up," said Philip.

"Sybil will probably know," said Bryde. "I will go and ask her."

She left them, and brother and sister were alone.

"Do you remember my warning, Philip?"

"About Reggie Mainwaring?"

"Yes. I am sure this has something to do with it."

Augusta slipped away to her room. A knock came to her door shortly afterwards; Philip had followed her.

"You are right, Gus; everything is at an end between Grisel and Jack."

"She was not worthy of him! I have always thought it," broke from Augusta impatiently.

Philip looked at her a moment attentively, and then said, just as he closed the door—

"You ought to know, I suppose. You and he were friends years ago."

Yes, it was truth. Years ago, they had been friends. Before the days of the Christmas-time at Hurst, when Augusta first grew up she met him, and he never knew the impression he had then made on the high-spirited girl. No other man had ever stirred the even tenor of her pulses. When Lenore first came on the scene, there had been a sharp struggle between pride and wounded love; but such womanish folly had long ago been cured, she thought. She affected rather to dislike men than otherwise, and still how strangely the news she had just heard upset her.

She acted simply on impulse when, shortly afterwards, on hearing Jack's door open at the other end of the passage, she met him on his way downstairs. He started when he saw her, and seemed surprised at her evident distress.

"I wanted to tell you how sorry I am for

you, Mr. Hunt. I couldn't bear to let you go and say nothing."

"Thank you, Miss Jerningham. Can I do anything for you in town?"

"How can you be so quiet about it all? If I were you I should have been miserable, and oh! so angry."

"Of what use were it? Such casualties all come in one's life's work."

"You were not always such a stoic, Mr. Hunt. When I first knew you, years ago, you felt like other mortals."

"Years ago that was. You are right. But the time since then has taught me philosophy as the only true good for humanity."

"Was that Miss Fenton's teaching?" She had uttered the words by what impulse she knew not.

"No," he answered, very quietly. "Lady Meredith's rule of life is a higher one than that. Fortunate are they who fall within the limits of her influence."

"I can see nothing different in her from other women. Give me the secret of her influence."

"I hardly know in what it lies; simply that she is herself, I think."

"Lord Meredith is a man to be envied."

"He is worthy of her, Miss Jerningham. But I must go, the dogcart will be at the door immediately."

"Good-bye, then. Will you take advice from me? Give yourself up to work. Make a name for yourself, and think no more of Grisel. A child could never have made you happy. She would only have held you back from fame."

"The philosopher cares not for fame; it is too ephemeral to satisfy him!"

"Why do you so carefully hide yourself? Do you think that *I* can ever believe you? Do you imagine that you can completely hide your feelings?"

"I do not pretend to do so; for this reason I tell you, when we meet next in the world of London, you will see that such things are good for me. I shall have laughed and grown fat on my diet of bitter herbs."

"And the Phyllis which serves them is a

child like Grisel! How *do* women have such influence? A baby with fair hair and laughing eyes can mar the life of a man!"

"It is still to be proved," he answered. "In the meanwhile, I must go."

She returned to her room. Philip was waiting in the hall, and drove Jack to the station.

"Mistake No. 2 in my life done with," he said, just as the train was starting. "I wonder what the next will be?"

The household at the Manor was an uncomfortable one that evening. Grisel did not leave her room, and there was an awkward silence amongst the others at the dinner-table. Mr. Romney was far from pleased at what had occurred, and blamed Sybil for not having spoken sooner. He could not endure to feel that one of his daughters had behaved ill to any man; and, besides, what excuse was to be given to the world at large?

Conversation came in spasmodic bursts, and all were thankful when the uncomfortable meal was at an end.

Two days after, Miss Griselda Romney received a letter by post. They were, as usual, at their summer quarters at Brighton. The letter was in her brother's handwriting; within, there was one also from Sybil.

Miss Griselda was alone at breakfast. The letters arrived before family prayers. She laid them on one side, much as she wished to know the subject on which he was writing.

The four trim maids left the room, and then she was at liberty to satisfy her curiosity.

"Well! I never in all my life heard of such a thing. It all comes of such unseemly haste."

She hurriedly left the room, and proceeded upstairs; she swept into her sister's room, in answer to the gentle invitation to come in.

"There have been nice doings at the Manor, Sybil. Grisel has refused to marry Mr. Hunt."

"My dear Griselda, there must be some mistake, some misunderstanding. A child like Grisel would never refuse. Do read it over carefully once more."

"Well, perhaps I am wrong in saying that she

refused to marry him, but it seems there is some absurd idea that she likes Reginald Mainwaring better, and Mr. Hunt heard it, and naturally he gave her up. I can hardly imagine any daughter of Thomas's, in fact any niece of ours, being in love with two men at once. After such a careful education, it seems to be so inexplicable and so very unlike what any of our family would have done."

"But surely it is better, Griselda, that the poor child discovered her mistake in time?"

"I am astonished, Sybil, at your leniency. A woman can never be excused any mistake she may make on such a grave subject. I am sure that we elder generation would never have done it."

"But remember, my dear, we were so different. We never were tried. We never even saw one man to like. Shut up as we were with our dear old father at the Manor, what temptations had we? I never remember even either of us having the slightest liking for anyone—flirtation they call it now-a-days."

N

"You may speak for yourself, Sybil. Of course in those days I was much younger than you. However, it is needless to revive old memories."

"Quite, my dear; fortunately I have none to revive. But what do they propose doing? Have she and Reginald come to an understanding?"

"I imagine the next thing you will ask is whether Reginald is to take Mr. Hunt's place at the altar—on the day previously settled. Really, Sybil, for the credit of the family, I trust she may not see him for years. I shall never be able to look any of our friends in the face again."

"Oh! my dear sister, if you only knew how thankful I am that she discovered it in time. Fancy how dreadful if it had happened, and she had found out afterwards that Reginald was first in her thoughts. I have seen so many loveless alliances. We must be thankful that our dearest Grisel has been spared. I think she should come at once to us, and we shall do our best to comfort her. She ought to leave home for a little. Thomas seems to be very much displeased."

"For once you have said a sensible thing, Sybil. Of course the child is but a child. Thomas is sure to be too harsh. Sybil will spoil her, besides being too young to act in such matters. She had much better come at once to us, and then a little judicious kindness and firmness will be best in every way for her. Of course you and I, Sybil, stand in the place of dear Thomas's wife to his daughters."

"Poor dears, I fear that two maiden aunts make but one inefficient mother."

"Better, at any rate, that they should have us than be left to the guidance of an over-indulgent father. It has always been dear Thomas's stumbling-block that he cannot see daylight for those three girls."

"Poor fellow, so young he was, too, to be left; and they are such good, sensible girls, they show how well he has brought them up."

"If such pleases you, by all means think it; but the present case is certainly one for a woman's management. How can an elderly man, entirely given up to his farm stock, have delicacy and sensibility enough to act on an occasion like the present? But I really must go and have some breakfast."

"Have you not had it yet, dear? And you will be sure to suffer from one of your nervous headaches, fasting so long."

"By-the-bye, there is another thing to be discussed, as I must write at once to Miss Tomlinson. You know my dress and bonnet were to be here the end of the week for the wedding. I cannot counter-order them, but I thought of sending her that black Chantilly of yours to substitute for my white lace; it will make the dress more useful, and you never use it."

"Welcome to it all, as you know. So long as it goes to the girls after my death, you may take what good you like out of it in the meanwhile."

"I believe you would give yourself away, if that were possible," said the younger Miss Romney, forgetting that she appropriated the possessions without any alarming amount of unwillingness.

So poor Grisel went down to Brighton. She rather alarmed her aunts at first from her excessive quietness, and willingness to do as she was told. A young lady who had had strength of mind to refuse to marry a man, and yet who took all the soup and "Allsopp" ordered for her, however much it went against her inclinations, was an anomaly to them. There was none of that firmness needed of which Miss Griselda had hoped such great things. Before a few days were over, they were both vying with each other as to spoiling her. Small tea parties were accepted, to which Grisel was led an unwilling victim ; and novels, an unheard-of indulgence for youth, were ordered from the library to try and rouse the child, she moped so.

For if truth be told, Grisel was longing to be at home again. She missed her sisters, and even though she had the comforting assurance in her own mind that Reggie cared for her, yet it was hard to know that he knew nothing of her feelings towards himself. Her father

positively refused to make any allusion to the
subject on the day of old Sir Roger's funeral.
So mother and son went abroad without hearing
of what happened; and Reggie daily studied
the *Times*, morbidly anxious to see for himself
the announcement of Grisel's marriage. They
were wandering from one place to another; and
though Reggie had promised to send their
address to the Manor when at last they should
come to a standstill, nothing had as yet been
heard of them.

So Grisel vegetated at Brighton during the
summer months, and thought much and often
of Jack. She wished so much that she could
hear of what he was doing. But no news came.
He had disappeared entirely out of her life; not
even keeping up a connecting medium through
Philip, his friend of many years' standing. He
felt it was better completely to give up all
communication with anyone who would either
be with the Romneys or be in such constant
correspondence with them.

So Grisel was not likely to have her wish for

news of him satisfied. After some months spent with her aunts, she returned home towards autumn, and fell once more into all her old ways. Constantly in attendance on her father, he at last forgave her, and as time went on, he let an occasional remark drop concerning the Mainwarings, or made some mild pleasantry which brought the colour to his daughter's face. So she came out of her moral corner, and counted the months till the year should have flown. Perhaps when Bramleigh was once more occupied her happiness would come.

But the girl could not forget Jack, though for ever lost to her. She felt she had left a scar on a man's life ; and she had meant no harm.

CHAPTER XIV.

FOR THE SAKE OF LONG AGO.

WE must return a few months. It was evening, the day after Jack left the Manor. The sun was streaming in at the windows of the Merediths' house in Prince's Gate, gay with its flower-boxes; a soft breeze was blowing, and the interiors of the rooms were cool and pleasant.

Lying on a sofa, so as to feel the influence of the air, was Lenore; she was gradually picking up her strength, and looked forward with unfeigned pleasure to the morrow, for she and her husband were leaving town for his seat in B——shire.

She was happier and brighter than she had been all the days of her married life; health was returning, and her spirits rose in consequence, and, added to all, duty was bringing its own reward; a very real love was growing up in her towards her husband, perhaps one that would stand the rubs and jars of daily existence better than even the early love of her girlhood.

She was thinking of days gone by, thinking also of Jack's wedding the following week, wishing it were over, and wondering much if Grisel would gain the influence over him that he so longed for; and even while she was so dreaming, the door opened, and Jack himself was announced.

"I thought you were at the Manor, Mr. Hunt. You are none the less welcome, however, from being an unexpected guest."

"I left the Manor last night very unexpectedly; but, Lady Meredith, before speaking of myself, let me hear how you are. I hardly thought I should have been admitted to-day. I hope my being so is a real indication that you are feeling better."

"Yes, I am gradually gaining strength, and look forward much to our flight from town to-morrow."

"What shall I do when you are gone?"

Jack spoke hopelessly, impatiently. Lenore could not understand his mood.

"You are the only woman that cares whether I go to the dogs or not. I feel as if I could throw it all up. I cannot grind on here alone; want of sympathy, want of all that makes life bearable, is driving me desperate."

"But what of Grisel?"

"Miss Romney is no longer anything to me. I have released her from her engagement—have set her free!"

"Free?"

Lenore could hardly believe that she heard aright. Was it freedom to Grisel that she had been released?

Thoughts crowded into her mind of what such freedom would have been for her. Silence was becoming dangerous; she dare not think of herself.

Jack was silent also; he had given no answer to her interrogation. He was sitting buried in thought, and moodily turning over the reels in

her workbox.   He was not aware of how close
it was to the edge of the table, neither knew
how it happened, but the box capsized, scattering
its contents far and wide.

Jack uttered many apologies for his carelessness,
and carefully collected the miscellaneous articles
together.

Lenore had the box on her knee, and was
rearranging the disturbed elements.   Suddenly
she seemed to miss something from its place,
and stopped to look for it.

"What is missing?   Do let me find it."

"Oh, it is nothing of any consequence; do not
trouble yourself any further."

But Jack, only too anxious to repair the mischief, was bent on search.   His hand came on
something; he raised it carefully, wondering what
it meant—a bow of some white ribbon, all charred
and burnt, and a fragment of some airy dress
material in the same condition.

Lenore had coloured painfully, trusting he
would connect nothing with her foolish relic.
When all else had been destroyed, it alone was

spared; she pleaded to herself that there was no harm in keeping a remembrance of her deliverer.

But Lenore's blushes were not needed to tell the tale. Jack rose to his feet with the charred fragment in his hand.

"That was a long time ago," he said, and replaced it in its hiding-place.

"You have never seen my boy," Lenore said, hurriedly, feeling anything would be better than being alone; "shall I send for him?"

"No; you must let me speak to you, Lady Meredith, and then I will see your boy. Can you listen while I speak? Can you bear with me while I tell you my story? You cannot say no, you must hear me, for the sake of that I found only a few moments ago, for the sake of the friendship you have promised is to be between us until death."

"Tell me, then, what has happened? How is it that you are once more anchorless in the world?"

"Lady Meredith, I learnt yesterday that though

I had never awakened in Grisel the love I craved for, another had done so. I was with her when she found out her mistake; nothing remained but that I should set her free."

"I suppose," said Lenore, thoughtfully, "such things happen to lead one onwards, upwards."

"Rather say to drag one downwards. How can a man rise morally if every help is denied to him? How can he believe in a Supreme Good when a Supreme Bad seems to be the stronger power in the world, and frustrates every struggle he makes in the right direction? I thought at last I was to find what I sought, and fate is absolutely relentless. Must one suffer all one's life through a false step made at the beginning of the day?"

"The false step *may* in the end lead one to higher things," said Lenore, earnestly. "Our desires are not gratified, not only because we desire them, but because if we had them we should rest content; and one dare not, one must not. Think of a human being such as you are, endowed with faculties above the average

of mind and body, craving for ever after something you have not, and at last finding that
'something' in human love, settling down and
gradually deteriorating, because your satisfaction
had been found in things of this world. No;
such can never be your life. I know you better
than you know yourself. I know that the future
still is yours, and you must not give in.

"But it is hard to fight on alone," he said,
wearily. "It is not good for man that such
should be; one is apt to grow selfish, self-
absorbed. Does not the world, do not women
raise the cry that man rarely lives exempt from
the sin? And yet you preach a lonely struggle
to me; and you, it is easy for you so to speak,
you are not alone in the world, half your burdens
are carried for you; you cannot understand what
I feel."

"Perhaps I cannot; perhaps I might myself
have failed in such a contest; but, Mr. Hunt—
oh, Jack, you must not give in. Forget these
mistakes; think only of your destiny as a man;
determine to live down this pain; turn to work,

if you will, in the meantime ; but remember, it too will fail you, though I should be so proud to feel you were making a name among your fellow-men ; and remember, though a worthy way of spending life, there must ever run through the stream a current tending to perfection not to be found here. Take as your motto, ' Excelsior.' "

"Oh, Lenore, if you had been beside me, I must have risen, and not fallen. I could not have breathed the air you breathed, I could not have shared your life, without the motive power extending itself even to me."

"I fear not ; it must be best as it is, or it would not be. I might have been a clog on you ; now, you have no earth-ties to draw you down, and I have found my happiness. My husband could not live without me ; I have grown to feel it is best."

"You have done the growing, and feel it is best ; I am at the other side, and still feel it is worst ; but as you say you have got over it, so can I, and so I will."

"Did I say it?" Lenore's voice was so low he did not hear, and then she continued aloud—

"I do not mean that you are to consider that this world can offer you no more of what is good, of what is worth struggling for; far from it. Man's life here may be noble, good, and humanly happy, but the flatter he lays the paving stones here, the more easily he will walk, the less will he bear the marks of the journey when he reaches the land that is very far off."

"How easy it sounds, and yet how hard in reality," was all that Jack said. He would like to have remained where he was for hours. Lenore might speak, and he would listen. He felt often as if he had nothing to say when she was there. How she had come to know him as she did he often wondered when he had told her so little of his real self; and yet he felt, when beside her, it was absolutely useless to hide behind a screen of indifference. That which had deceived others had never deceived her.

A man's horror of showing that he ever felt at all was stronger in him than in most. If he had

married Lenore in the old days, he could not
long have hidden his true self.   Now it was
doubtful whether anyone would ever break the
barrier down.   Probably not; probably, even if
he did marry in the future, his wife would know
as little of his inner life as the world outside.
One woman only could have unlocked the door.

"Well," he said at last, "I fear I must go,
Lady Meredith, or my visit will have done you
harm."

Lenore roused herself from the reverie into
which she had fallen.

"Do not go yet; I want to hear what your
plans are.   You were going to have had some
holiday.   You will not give up the idea?"

"I half think of going a walking tour on the
Continent somewhere—do some Alpine climbing
perhaps, and then come home and settle down
to work."

"Perhaps, when you return, you will pay us
a visit.   Lord Meredith will be so glad if you
could arrange to be with us in autumn, and get
some shooting."

o

"I should like it above all things. May I let you know when I return from my Continental wanderings?"

"I was going to ask you to do so, and, if you have time, let us hear how you get on. You must remember that you are not altogether solitary, and that at any rate there is one house at which news of your doings will be always welcome."

Jack rose to go, and held out his hand.

"Will you be glad to hear that if I ever come to any good I have to thank you for it? The knowledge that she has guided a man towards good, even though he never attains it, must be a continual happiness to a woman. You said once you would throw the rope that would save a man, and you have kept your word. May the rope be strong enough to draw such a drowning man to shore."

"It must," she said.

So they parted—Jack to his Alpine wanderings, Lenore to her daily life.

When he left her that afternoon, she fell into

a dream about him. How she longed that in some way his life might be brightened, even though the happiness came to him in a way that would cut her friendship off! She had not wished it at first; now she could say truly that she did not care if she had aught to do with it, so long as he was truly happy.

And in the days and weeks which followed, as she wandered among the woods and fields, and enjoyed to the full her country life, and felt health steadily returning, her thoughts often turned to Jack, tracing his way in his travels, trying to unravel the tangled web of his story, wondering what the future held in store for him.

CHAPTER XV.

THE RIVER ONCE MORE.

A LARGE coffee-room in a well-known hotel at a small town on the shores of the Lago di Maggiore.

The hour is that of breakfast, and hurried waiters flutter from table to table trying to supply the wants of exigeant travellers.

The *persiennes* are closed, the room feels cool and refreshing; the butter lying in ice, the plates of tempting fruit and cool, green leaves, invite one to refresh oneself. Outside various vehicles are standing, horses stamping and fretting from the flies, luggage is being piled on; some are going farther south, others are retracing their footsteps across the Alps.

By degrees the wants of all are supplied. One table alone remains unoccupied. Two places are set, and a waiter still hovers round, attending to the preparations for breakfast.

The large glass swing doors open, heads turn from the various tables and scan with curiosity the young Englishman who enters, calmly reading *Galignani*, as if no eyes were bent upon him. The waiter rushes forward and conducts him to the table in reserve, and, as he seats himself, he orders the coffee to be brought.

Reggie Mainwaring—for he it is—sits down calmly and waits. Lady Mainwaring presently enters, looking more charming than ever in her widow's dress.

How well both are looking, how perfectly happy they seem to be together! He is reading to her scraps of home letters.

" It is so strange that we have had no letter from Sybil. I almost thought we should have heard something of Grisel and Jack, even if we had not met."

It was Lady Mainwaring who spoke.

"I have looked in all the visitors' books, and can find their names nowhere. It seems odd we never saw the announcement of the marriage," Reggie answered.

"Yes, very strange. They must have been abroad for more than a month now, and I am sure there was some talk of their coming as far south as this."

"We may meet still," said Reggie; but his voice hardly sounded full of anticipation.

His mother looked at him, and drew a long breath. She wondered when he would forget Grisel, and the night which had been so full of sadness beside his father's deathbed.

But, as often happens in this world, the words were scarcely out of Reggie's mouth when the doors once more opened to admit a single figure.

The Mainwarings looked at each other, but neither spoke. They had not been recognised by Jack Hunt when he entered. He was giving some directions about his luggage and a guide.

He was just starting for some Alpine expedition. Then he turned round and coolly surveyed the occupants of the different tables. A start, a half inclination to leave the room; and stepping forward, he held out his hand.

"This is an unexpected meeting," he said.

A few words passed between them. Jack asked of their movements, carefully avoiding his own.

Then Lady Mainwaring put the question that her son dare not.

"Where is La Grise? I hope she will be here soon, as we are just starting on our travels, and we should like to see her."

"Have you not heard? But you must have done so. Have you had no letters from the Manor?"

"None. We have been wondering at their silence; but we expect to hear from Sybil to-day or to-morrow. We gave her Stresa as an address to write to."

"She will explain all to you. Good-bye."

"You are alone here?" asked Reggie, suppressing the eagerness of his tones.

"Alone! Grisel is at the Manor;" and without more explanation he was gone.

Half-an-hour afterwards they saw him pass the window in a carriage *en route* for Switzerland, and then a note was brought to Reggie.

He read it slowly through, and handed it to his mother.

"It is from Jack. Poor fellow!"

Lady Mainwaring read as follows :—

"I could not give the explanation which, though a sad one to me, must be full of happiness to you. Go home and win Grisel Romney; she loves you, and I have set her free.

"J. H."

Nothing more but the bare fact stated.

Long they talked over the strange announcement, and eagerly they watched for Sybil's letter, which, when it came, only brought the news of the engagement between her sister and Mr. Hunt being at an end, but giving no reason how such had come to pass.

Reggie wished to start for home at once; but such could not be. His mother's health had to be considered, and then he could not return and take up the happiness that had just been wrenched from another man, and that man, rival though he had been, he had always liked. So he put aside his impatience, and wrote a long letter to Sybil—told her of their meeting with Jack, and asked for an explanation.

So the weeks ran on, and at last Sybil's answer came; but it begged Reggie not to hurry home. It was of no use, she said; she did not think her father would let any engagement take place for some months to come, and Grisel knew nothing of his letter.

But in autumn Bramleigh was once more occupied. The Romneys had no warning of the Mainwarings' return; Reggie wished it kept secret, and mother and son were fully established before their nearest neighbours knew anything of it. They arrived at the end of the week, but the family pew was not filled at morning service next day.

The day passed as all other Sundays at the Manor did. The family, in full force, had inspected the live stock in every direction; afternoon tea was over, and they had dispersed to spend the time according to their several inclinations.

Grisel slipped away alone. She had received a letter that day from Augusta Jerningham which made her think. Augusta's letters were always amusing and full of gossip, but a different tone ran through this one. She seemed to be having a pleasant summer, and she was going to pay the Merediths a visit. Her letter was full of anticipations, and Grisel wondered; she had not known that Lady Meredith was such a favourite with Augusta.

"We are to have a houseful," Augusta wrote, "and you will be glad to hear that Mr. Hunt is to be of the party. He has just returned from the Continent. I met him in town the

other day.   He is looking very well; he has
evidently thriven on your treatment.   He told
me he had met the Mainwarings abroad.   So
let me give you a piece of advice, Grisel.
Don't fret about the past.   You and he were
wise in what you did, and I am sure he knows
it."

What a problem Jack had always been to
Grisel!   She had not attempted the solution
thereof in the years that were past, but somehow
now she longed to read the riddle.

She felt sure it was for the best that they
had parted.   She understood now how little she
had really known of him.   He came suddenly
into her life; she knew nothing of him before
then; in a fortnight's time she was engaged to
him, and for four years so it had been, and
then as suddenly she had lost sight of him,
and his whole existence must ever be to her an
unsolved riddle.

When next she heard of him, he was amusing
himself as if she had never been.   Had he ever
really cared for her?

Grisel had wandered some way from home, and was slowly wending her way towards Bramleigh along the river's side.

It was towards the middle of October, and woods and ferns were clothed in russet and gold. The leaves were beginning to fall, and formed a many-coloured carpet, while the only life to be seen was in the pheasants as they fled across the path at her approach, and took refuge in the neighbouring cover.

Grisel came to a pause at length. She felt tired; she had walked farther than she had intended to do on first setting out. She looked at her watch—it was still early; she could not make up her mind to return home, it was such a perfect afternoon; so, scrambling down the bank, she found a nook by the water's side where she could rest.

A perfect hiding-place from any chance passer-by—seen only from the river—Grisel was quite happy in her corner. The river was full of association to her, and she went over again the many strange adventures she had had on it, always accompanied by the same companion. She read many things now that had happened by a different light, and wondered how before she had been so blind.

A willow stretched its feathery drapery into the water beyond her, and a tangle of grasses and sedges completed her leafy screen. The water-hens dived and swam about, enjoying to the full their feast of insects with which the air teemed, and Grisel sat, as she thought, in solitary possession of the scene ; but the water-hens had quicker ears than she had, for they darted into their hiding-places along the banks, and then, wondering at their discomposure, she listened, and nearer and nearer came the sound of oars in the water ; some one was coming quickly down the stream.

Grisel could not see what intruder approached, but the flutter of her dress must have been visible through the willow boughs, for in another minute a boat shot round the corner, guided directly to her hiding-place. It was Reggie.

"I thought I should find you here. I came in search of you. Will you come with me a little way, La Grise?"

Grisel had sprung to her feet, in her first glad surprise, and held out her hands.

"When did you come back, Le Gris? No one is expecting you!"

"So no one is glad to see me. Never mind, Grisette; you must forgive my return. Some one said something once about a bad penny, and I suppose I am to be thought of in the same way."

Reggie drew to shore, and Grisel stepped into the boat. It all seemed so natural, she could hardly believe how long the time had been since last they met.

Reggie spoke of many things, trying to distract her mind from the pain of their last meeting. He had much to tell her of their travels, and much to hear of the Romneys' doings.

"Tom is salmon-fishing in Scotland, or rather has been, and is now travelling about."

"And when does he return home?"

"Oh! he must be here within the next six weeks. Bryde's marriage is to be then."

"Where is Philip just now?" asked Reggie, paying no attention to Grisel's last statement.

"Hard at work in Yorkshire; he likes the life immensely, and Bryde has screeds of description in consequence. She is looking forward to the kind of life she will lead very much; but, Reggie, I shall miss her dreadfully; we have always been together."

"And what will Sybil do?"

"I don't know. She has her painting, and I have nothing, you know."

The oars ceased their rapid stroke, and the boat went lazily along with the stream.

"I wonder, La Grise, if Sybil would miss you as much as you will miss Bryde?"

"Me! Why?"

"I was wondering what the Manor would be like without you, that was all."

"A very foolish wonder indeed, Le Gris. You

had much better employ your time in thinking of realities."

"Speculating of the future, Grisette. Do you never do it?"

Reggie watched to see the effect his words would have, but she turned away her head.

"Take care," she exclaimed, "you will run us aground;" and, in truth, they were very near the landing pier at the Manor.

"You will come up to the house and see them all, Le Gris? They would be disappointed if you did not do so, and you have plenty of time."

"Yes; I am coming. Take care, now; I am going to help you out to-day, Grisette, even though your hands are free."

"Don't, Le Gris," she exclaimed, for he had taken both her hands in his, and he had the advantage, for she still stood in the boat and he on *terra firma*."

"Now, Grisette, listen a moment! May I ask Sybil if she would miss you very much?"

"Of course she would miss me," said Grisel.

"She will have to make up her mind to it, my queen. I need you more than Sybil. Will you come to me, La Grise?"

"Yes, Le Gris, if you wish it; and Sybil will not mind very much, I think."

P

CHAPTER XVI.

CONCLUSION.

THIS story is nearly told ; one more scene yet remains, and after that the history of the actors that figure in these pages can be traced no further, for their future lies still before them as well as our own, and though there is such a thing as surmise as to how they will fulfil their destinies, no certain facts can be told of that which has not yet come to pass.

Some four or five years have passed since the events related in the last chapter, and we are back at The Hurst once more.

Mr. and Mrs. Wyld have, as in the old days, a houseful, and the Merediths are among the guests, otherwise the gathering is composed of strangers, Mrs. Wyld being afraid of recalling painful associations to Lenore regarding her first visit when her father was alive and with her.

Lenore and her husband have been out walking, and she has been showing him her old haunts. They are returning homewards now; it is late in the day, and Mrs. Wyld is coming to Lenore's room for a chat before dinner.

Lenore looks well and happy as she walks lightly along, with her hand within her husband's arm, though she does not now need it for support.

It is winter-time, and the cold, frosty air has brought colour to her face. She is speaking eagerly to him as they approach, and he is all attention to what she is saying. The years have left but little trace on either of them. Time sometimes deals kindly.

"So now you know all about it, Fred, and you must put all thought of it out of your foolish old head."

"And be very thankful that the present is

mine, Lenore. Child, what you have told me this afternoon is like yourself; you have raked up the ashes of the past to relieve my mind. I shall ever thank you for it."

"If I had known years ago that you were fretting about an unexplained something, I should have spoken; but I thought you knew nothing, and that it was best to leave you in ignorance, when I could prove to you from hour to hour what goodness you had brought into my life. You understand what I mean, Fred? And now are you content to let the Past be buried, for the Present is ours?"

"And the Future! Lenore, what can I say to convince you of my happiness, save that the wish rises at times that this life were eternal?"

"Life is eternal," she answered, very low, "and so is love."

Neither spoke again till, as they passed the house, they heard a burst of childish laughter and a patter of childish feet at play in the oak corridor.

"I must go to him, Fred, for a little before Mrs. Wyld takes possession of me. Will you spare me?"

"I suppose I must, Lenore. When do you think he will be old enough to send to school?"

Lord Meredith was always teazing his wife about such a change.

But she gave no reply.

It was half-an-hour later when Mrs. Wyld invaded Lenore's room, bright with the ruddy glow of firelight.

"Now this is comfortable, Lenore. Do not move, and I shall draw in this chair to the fire. The post has just arrived, and brings me a varied correspondence, and also a letter for you."

Lenore glanced at the writing by the fire-light.

"It is from Mr. Hunt," she said; "he promised to write to me soon."

"How strange! and I was just going to tell you he has been winning laurels in the literary world. He was always such a favourite of mine, I feel quite sunning myself in his reflected glory."

"Yes; before we left town, people were beginning to talk. He throws himself so much into his work that he deserves to succeed."

"But he hates any allusion to the subject, I find," said Mrs. Wyld. "He has grown so reserved within the last few years; he requires a wife to smooth out the creases, and I have a deep-laid plan in my head to turn matchmaker."

"Take care," said Lenore, smiling, "it rarely succeeds."

"Oh, but this must do so. I shall have them both here together, and you know they were old loves before Miss Romney, now Lady Mainwaring, came on the scene; besides, the girl has softened down immensely within the last few years. I really think Augusta Jerningham would make him a very good wife."

"I do not think Mr. Hunt will ever marry," said Lenore, thoughtfully.

" So Mr. Wyld says," answered that worthy's wife, " but you know one can never count on men, and that is the only subject on which my husband and I differ."

Marcus Ward & Co., Printers, Royal Ulster Works, Belfast.